BOOTHEADS

MO JOHNSON

**WALKER
BOOKS**

First published in Great Britain 2010 by Walker Books Ltd
87 Vauxhall Walk, London SE11 5HJ

2 4 6 8 10 9 7 5 3 1

Text © 2008 by Mo Johnson

Cover photo © Fotosearch/Photolibrary.com

This book has been typeset in Amasis MT

Printed and bound in Great Britain by Clays Ltd, St Ives plc

British Library Cataloguing in Publication Data:
a catalogue record for this book is
available from the British Library

ISBN 978-1-4063-2592-8

www.walker.co.uk

1

Change tiptoed into our lives with her eyes down, like a shy chick coming late to class. We checked her out, as you do, and found nothing there worth bothering about. Too many other hot girls were standing in line and Casey, Ed and I had our hands full. If we'd deemed her worthy of a second glance, we might have noticed the ruthless determination in her eyes. We may even have asked what she had planned for us, but we ignored her and that was our biggest mistake.

Not that she cared. She just went right on doing her thing. We didn't even see her coming, especially not on the day that Ed stood over me, his tanned shoulders blocking out the light.

"You played like a girl out there, Tommo." He scowled.

I eyed him steadily. Don't break the stare. Never break the stare. Casey joined him. Between them they had my escape route covered.

"Didn't he, Casey? Didn't he play like a chick?"

Casey moved in closer. "Yeah," he taunted, his towel hovering above my bare thigh.

I knew what he was about to do and so did Ed. As Casey held the towel taut with both hands, Ed lunged at me, pinning me down. In an instant, a flash of white cotton snapped at my flesh, stinging viciously. I struggled hard against Ed as Casey raised his hands again.

"Like a big…"

Swipe.

"Fat…"

Swipe.

"Chick!"

Casey poised himself for another attack but I managed to break free in time to catch the towel before it landed.

"Well, you'd be the expert on big fat chicks, Casey. How many kilos did your girlfriend pile on last week?" I hissed, yanking the towel from his grip as I stood up.

"Lena's not fat," he protested.

"Face it, mate." I shoved him out of my way. "We're talking bush pig."

"It's comfort eating," Ed said. "Going out with Casey's depressing her."

"You're supposed to be on my side right now, Ed," Casey reminded him.

"The Edster takes no sides," Ed announced.

Casey flashed me a grin just before we both crash tackled The Edster to the ground.

"Do you really think Lena's put on weight?" Casey demanded as he offered Ed a hand.

Ed sprang to his feet and headed to the shower.

"Blown up like a balloon."

"Should I dump her?"

"You've only been seeing her for a couple of months," Ed said, closing his cubicle door.

"Exactly! So I'm not attached to her, am I? I mean, if she can beef up this much in a few months, God knows what she'll look like by summer. I'm not hanging with a porker on the beach."

"Do you hear that, Ed? Casey's not surfing with you this summer," I yelled, thumping on his door as I passed. It flew open at once.

"Get real!" A nude Ed sucked his gut in a bit further and flexed his arms. "Check out these guns. This is solid muscle."

Casey and I were laughing too hard to respond.

"Seriously," he argued, "look at these pecs. That's what a gym does for you."

"I don't think a couple of Thursday night visits count."

"Hey! Me and some players from the Bombers have been going for ages."

"First I've heard," I said.

"I don't tell you two everything, you know. Anyway, these guys have got all the info on the club's talent development officer. The word is he's going round checking out the local college games this month."

"Glad you're getting something out of your visits then," Casey snorted, squeezing Ed's upper arm.

Ed shrugged him off. "It's doing more for me, Casey, than it is for Lena."

9

"Lena's going there?" Casey asked.

"Yeah ... she gives her mouth a real good workout, chatting up all the instructors."

I laughed.

"Shut up, you two. Lena's not fat, she's curvy," Casey protested again.

"She was fat when you met her," I said bluntly.

"No way, man!"

"She was," Ed agreed, returning to his shower and kicking the door shut again.

Casey looked dismayed. "Why didn't anyone tell me?"

"What would you have done if we had? Dumped her right away?" Ed called.

"Nah," Casey conceded, "I'd have seen her in secret till I got laid and then I'd have dumped her."

"So, I guess if that's your plan, you'll be dating her for a while then?" Ed yelled over the swish of water.

"Well, smart arse, if you must know ... I could have dumped her last weekend."

I spun round. "No. Way."

Ed launched himself out of the shower again, bowling Casey over. This time he was wearing a film of soap.

I joined the Casey assault. "You're winding us up," I said, twisting a handful of Casey's guts.

"Are you?" Ed yelled, struggling with him on the wet tiles.

"No! Get off me, you're dripping wet!"

"ARE YOU?" Ed yelled louder and sat on Casey's chest while I kept up the Chinese burning.

"No!" He was laughing hard as he pummelled Ed's bare chest. Good job no one was hanging around with a camera phone. After a few seconds of pain, he gave in. "Oh, piss off then. I'll be seeing her for another week, I guess."

"You mean another year!" Ed punched the air in triumph. "I knew it. There's no way you were getting laid before me, man. Not with these pecs."

"Or me," I added.

"Yeah, right. I have a better chance of getting some than you lot, and you know it. You two losers haven't even got chicks to call your own."

Ed snorted as he returned to the still running shower. He let out a cry. "Bloody hell, the water's freezing now."

"Serves you right. Your chick problems boil down to two simple facts," said Casey.

I took the bait. "Yeah? What?"

"You're too fussy, Tommo, and Ed's too ugly."

"We're working on it, aren't we, Ed?" I entered my cubicle.

"We are?" Ed shouted.

"Rhona Smith's party. No parents. Plenty of chicks full of grog. It'll be the end of the drought, mate."

"It will?"

"It bloody better be." I twisted the hot tap carefully.

"Well, take a paper bag for your ugly heads, just in case. Or put one over Amy Jones's head and chat her up." Casey roared and his voice echoed off the locker room walls.

"I'm not that desperate."

"Yet!" Casey called back.

Ed's shower stopped abruptly. I closed my eyes and savoured the trickle of water on my skin.

"So Tommo, did we mention that you played footy like a chick out there?" Ed thumped on the door of my cubicle.

"A big fat chick," Casey agreed.

I grinned and turned the taps on full.

2

I couldn't get Lena Hughes out of my head on the way home from footy practice. There are a lot of stick insect girls in our year and yeah, flat abs are cool, but what's the point if there's nothing to balance them in the tit department? Lena's got great tits but she doesn't have flat abs. She's got a roll there. I've seen it straining through her white school shirt. I've watched her suck it in whenever Casey is around. The girl has some serious lung capacity there and it's all good for me because when she sucks in her gut for hours on end, her boobs pop out even more. Then there's that long black hair that curls in a pattern across her forehead, round her ears and through her fingers when she tries to tame it. It's sexy.

She reckons she's loved Casey forever, but I can't see how that can be true because she was going out with Brad Sweetman in Year Ten and he reckons he screwed her last year, but no one believes him. Maybe that's because he also reckons that his dad apparently went to school with Nicole Kidman and screwed her on a school camp to Tasmania back in the eighties. I asked Mum about that and she laughed her head off.

"Honestly, Tommy, if I had a dollar for every low-life who claims to have the dirt on our A-list here in Australia, I'd be rich. Trust me, Nicole Kidman did not sleep with some zitty adolescent on a field trip to Tassie, darling. Unfortunately for the press, our Nic is one hundred per cent clean… Lord knows we've been digging deep enough for years."

I believe her. She works in the media. Gossip is her life.

I wondered briefly if Mum may have actually cooked dinner for once tonight but I abandoned this dream in favour of Lena again. I suppose she does have a sizeable bum, there's no getting away from that, but it's the kind you want to squeeze as opposed to yelling out, "Eclipse! Run for your life!" I reckon she's more than cute and I'm sure Ed thinks so too, although I've never asked him.

"Tommy, is that you?" Mum yelled out from her study as I slammed the front door. Who else would it be? Dad's been in Europe for three weeks now.

"No, it's not me," I said, sticking my head through her doorway. "Jeez, it's a mess in here, Mum."

She tugged at her blond ponytail. "Tell me about it. Just over a week left until the launch and nothing's going right. How did the game go?"

"We won. I played like a champion."

"Well, there's a first time for everything."

I laughed. "How would you know? You don't have a clue about footy."

"Yes, you're right. I loathe it! Oh, if only you'd been a girl, Tommy," she sighed over the top of her new Gucci glasses. I know they're Gucci because she's told me a thousand times. Actually, I reckon I know a lot more than even the average chick about designer fashion and stuff like that. How could I not, with a mum like mine?

"I really need a girl around here." Her eyes twinkled through the tiny red frames.

"Me too, and she'd be in the kitchen fixing our dinner right now instead of me having to phone for takeaway. It is take-away again, isn't it?"

"I fancy Thai. A beef salad, extra mild."

"Right then." I headed out the door, accidentally stomping on a tube of squishy stuff that had been tossed carelessly on her floor.

"Tommy," she yelped, her eyes wide with horror. She jumped up. "It's gone all over my Jeffrey Anderson."

Looking down at the rug, I could see that. What I didn't know was what *it* was, exactly. Brown make-up of some sort, and who the hell was Jeffrey Anderson? Probably some rip-you-off interior designer.

"Mum, people who buy white fluffy rugs are doomed to a life of disappointment," I said, resisting the urge to wipe the stuff off my shoe right there.

"What is this crap anyway?"

"It's a new cover-up product, Tommy. We're reviewing it in the first edition of *PINK*, or at least we planned to until you came along."

"What does it cover up?"

"Spots, blemishes … rugs … that kind of thing."

I looked back down at the unnatural coloured gunk.

"You'd need to be an orange for it to work."

She sighed. "Tommy, most females know that—"

"Yeah, yeah, yeah. Do you want me to clean it up or not?"

"Lord, no. You've done enough damage. Just go hunt for food, child."

I crossed the room, stepping over several other obstacles en route to the door, and headed for the kitchen.

"Tommy?" Mum called from her study. "Can you get that?"

The phone was ringing.

"What line?" I shouted. This house has more lines than the White House. Actually, I don't really know how many lines the White House has but I figure it has to be a lot.

"Our private line," she called back.

It was Dad.

"Hey, Tommy, how are things?"

"Fine."

"Did your team win today?"

He never forgets a thing, my dad.

"Yeah."

"You play well?"

I lied, of course.

"Good stuff, mate. Put your mum on. Is she all right? How's the new magazine coming along?"

"What do you think? With a name like *PINK* she can't go wrong," I said.

"Not long to the launch. Is she stressed?"

"Judge for yourself."

"MUM!" I yelled, but she was right beside me.

"Dad?" Her eyebrows were raised.

I nodded.

As she took the phone, smiling, she mouthed "Dinner?" and pointed to the door.

I gave her the thumbs up and grabbed my jacket.

"Disaster, Peter," she was telling him as I headed out.

She listened to his response then added, "No, the magazine is fine. It's my Jeffrey Anderson. Tommy has only gone and put a sample of concealer all over it."

Dad was making suitably sympathetic noises, I'm sure.

"Oh, he was trying to hide a huge zit on his chin," she told him. "I caught him trying on the lippy sample too." She winked at me. "But scarlet's just not his colour."

I rolled my eyes in mock outrage and left. I was still smiling as I reached the gate. I guess, all up, my life was pretty good. If only I'd known how to appreciate it then.

3

Monday mornings are bad enough without having to cope with double English first up.

"Why is the letter from Mr Darcy so significant?" Mrs Lennon was standing next to Casey and me, but she was addressing the entire class. She picked up Casey's pen lid and twiddled it absently in her fingers.

"What letter?" Casey whispered.

I shrugged. "I haven't read it yet."

"What? I thought you watched the DVD."

"I did but I fell asleep. Dunno about a letter."

He was annoyed. "Mate, you said you'd watch it for us."

"I couldn't get into it." *Pride and Prejudice*. Mrs Lennon says it's a "classic" but I much prefer Casey's take on it: a "boring chick book about boring chicks, written by a dead chick."

"Well, you should have given it a go. Now we're both in the shit."

"Tom?" Mrs Lennon faced us. I tried stalling her with a

pensive, "*I'm considering your question deeply*" look, but I was busted.

"And I suppose I'd be completely wasting my time asking you for an answer, Steven Casey?"

She flicked the pen lid at him. It bounced off his tie and onto the floor. She didn't bat an eyelid.

We opted for the "*charming grin*" move as a poor second, both reaching down to pick it up. I got to it just as Casey overreached and went tumbling off his chair. The class erupted.

Mrs Lennon stood her ground but I could see creases of suppressed laughter around her eyes, through her silver-framed glasses. Mrs Lennon's a good teacher but she's not hot like Ed's teacher, Miss Flannery, the newly-qualified chick who has the bottom class. Ed's in there because too much footy has damaged his brain. You can't be the best player in the school without making some sacrifices. I expect they gave Miss Flannery the dumb classes just in case she was a rubbish teacher, hoping that the kids wouldn't notice and knowing that even if they did, no one would care. But Ed reckons she's good and guys all over the school have been pretending to be dumb just to get themselves moved into her class.

Casey's diversionary tactic, drastic though it was, seemed to work on Mrs Lennon.

"Tell them, Amy." She sighed in good-hearted exasperation as she turned away from us.

We both looked round at Amy Jones who sat about two rows behind us. I couldn't see what Casey was doing; it's really hard to see when you're pulling crossed eyes, but I knew it had to be equally stupid from the contemptuous look Amy threw us before answering the question.

"Well, Miss, I think you'd agree that … *blah … blah…*"

Amy Jones, what a piece of work! Think of the most up-herself chick you know and Amy Jones could be her teacher. Every withering look makes you feel totally dumb; every smart answer comes out so fast you just can't get the reply to form in your mouth; every piercing stare puts your brain under a microscope and makes you feel she knows exactly what you're thinking. Amy Jones invented all those moves and she's out there passing them on to girls everywhere. She's the face of pure evil! She's…

"Great tits."

I turned, startled. Casey was in my ear.

I considered them for a moment before coming to my senses. What was I thinking? This was no ordinary female. She was a mean mouth on legs!

"Exactly, Amy." Mrs Lennon turned back to us again and smiled pointedly.

"And I really think Tom and Steve can learn from that. In fact, most males can," she teased, to the delight of the girls in the room and finally headed back down the front.

Kieran Donnelly put his hand up. "So are you saying that none of us could write a letter like that?" He looked at the boys for backup. "Come on, all those Darcy guys were just the same as us. They knew what girls wanted to hear and they wrote it. It's not that hard."

"That is assuming you know your alphabet, Kieran,"

Rhona Smith quipped and even the people who didn't find it funny forced out a laugh. Everyone wanted a party invitation.

"So you don't think that men were more sensitive back then? Better educated? More in tune with women?" Mrs Lennon lobbed the questions like grenades.

"No way!" Most of the boys were exploding but finding it hard to be heard over the females who were all agreeing with the teacher.

"I think it was their culture that makes it seem that way," I hesitated, trying to find the words, struggling to remember the Mr Darcy on the DVD.

"Go on, Tom."

"I mean, they were so polite, weren't they? They had to write letters and stuff because they weren't really allowed to talk to women. They couldn't."

"Oh and you can?" Amy guffawed. "You wouldn't have a clue about how to talk to a woman, Tom."

I ignored her.

Casey didn't. "How would you know, Jonesy? You don't qualify as a woman. You're a—"

Mrs Lennon held up her hand. "That'll do, you two."

But Amy got the last word in as usual. "I think Steve's just proved my point, Miss."

Rhona high-fived her and they sniggered. I elbowed Casey in annoyance.

"What?" He glared at me and muttered, "Rhona's a bitch too. Let's boycott her party."

"As if!" I spluttered, then I tried addressing the class again.

"All I'm saying is that we're always having to think about contexts and stuff in English, aren't we?"

Mrs Lennon nodded with an approving smile.

Excellent. I was on a roll.

"I just think the setting makes everything seem different to us now. I mean, English society, hundreds of years ago? Come on, it's another world, but I don't think men and women have changed that much really."

"If I were to drop you back into that time, Tom, do you think that you'd fit right in?" Mrs Lennon's eyes twinkle when she's debating a point with anyone, but when she really likes what she's hearing they switch to high beam.

Encouraged, I continued. "Yeah, I think I would … once I'd learned a bit about the customs and the culture and…"

"And read the book." Casey coughed.

"Once you've learned about women, you mean."

I spun round to face Amy. She was really starting to bug me now.

"Look, Amy, women are so not the big deal they think they are. I know you love all your 'women from Jupiter, men from Mars' crap."

"You mean, women from Venus, men from Uranus?"

The class seemed to groan and laugh at the same time.

Amy held her hand up. "I know, I know … crap joke, sorry." She was nodding her head, inviting forgiveness, which she seemed to be getting from people who were laughing harder now. Even Casey was grinning.

I scowled. "Face it, Amy." My raised voice cut through

the chaos and everyone fell silent. "You're not that difficult to work out. With your gossip, your obsession with other girls' looks, your obsession with your own looks and all that fashion stuff..." I was starting to forget my own point. The whole class was staring at me. I made an effort to concentrate again and nailed it! "Build a bridge and sashay over it in your Manolo Blankets. You're no big mystery."

Ha! Aced her!

I could tell that all the girls were impressed by my knowledge of designer shoes. *Thanks, Mum.* I leaned back casually in my chair, being careful not to do a Casey.

"I agree, Tom." Amy was smiling. Her lips were full and they kind of glistened. I found myself wondering what they would taste like.

Mean mouth, mean mouth! Hold it together, man.

Finally, my brain overruled my balls. Amy agreeing with me was not a good sign. And why were most of the girls now snorting with laughter?

"Some guys do get it, some guys even know their shoes from their manchester, Tommo, but evidently not you."

Manchester? How come were we suddenly talking about English soccer? She was infuriating. She just had to have the last word and she always threw it in right when you thought she had nothing. Right when your winning words have just left the battlefield to party. All you can do is stand at the door and call them back, "Oi, you guys, it's not over yet. Get your helmets back on!" But they've already gone ... and so are you!

I opened my mouth in an attempt to get back into it but she had this superior little smirk on her face, probably meant to intimidate me. It worked. I shut up.

Thank God for Mrs L.

"Fine. That's almost time and we've had an interesting discussion." She snapped her book closed, looking bemused. "I think for homework I'm going to set you all a little challenge. I want each person to choose a member of the opposite sex in this class and write a letter in which you praise one aspect of his or her personality. All letters must be complimentary. And Steve, if you haven't got anything nice to say, make it up. After all, you guys seem to be arguing that you can flatter a woman just as effectively today as the men could in Jane Austen's time, so a little creative complimenting shouldn't be too difficult."

"Do we need to use formal English?" Amy asked.

"Nah ... write it in Spanish." Casey guffawed at his own bad joke.

"Shut up," I hissed, seeing the contemptuous looks the girls were throwing him.

"What?"

"She said *formal* English, you tosser."

The smile died on his face.

"So I guess you won't be writing your letter to her then?"

"What do you think?" He paused for a second and his eyes began to glint. "Hey, Tommo, I dare you to write to her."

"Are you kidding me?"

"No, seriously, man. How hard would it be to flatter her?

It would be impossible, which really means that what you've been saying this lesson is total bullshit."

I thought about that and raised my hand. "Miss, do we give these letters to the person or do we give them to you?"

"Give them to me with your name on the top so I can check that you've done what I asked. Address your person by name and sign it Mr Darcy or Elizabeth Bennett, that way no one but you and I will know who wrote what when I read them out. I'll assess them all individually but I'll read out a few samples in class. And handwrite them, please. Mr Darcy didn't have a computer."

"Right, you're on," I told Casey. "Amy will never expect me to write to her. She knows we hate her guts. Hey, how much do you want to bet I can have her running after me by Rhona's party?" I was amazed we'd got through a whole lesson without her party being whispered about, except by Casey and me. It was the hot topic of every other lesson.

"No way!" Casey was shoving his books into his bag. "But if there's any sign of a meltdown with that ice queen, I'll shout you the next Ziggy's."

I forced myself to stop ogling the party girl who looked hot as she bent over the desk gathering up her stuff.

"You already owe me the next Ziggy's."

"Well, the one after that then."

I pushed my chair under the desk and tried to come up with a payment more appealing than a Big Zigg hamburger meal deal, but he was out the door before I could catch him.

4

When I did eventually find Casey again, he was in Ziggy's. It's the closest thing this povo suburb has got to a McDonald's. In fact, McDonald's should sue them for totally ripping off every idea they have. Most school days we're in there by three-twenty; Casey and I eat the food, Ed cooks it.

I was already chomping on chicken nuggets when Casey reached the table with a kids' Zigglet Meal: hamburger, small fries, Coke and, of course, the toy. Casey has collections of the things going right back to when he was a little kid.

"What're you doing out here?" I asked as Ed suddenly appeared behind Casey.

"Having a break." Ed yawned, tugging at a fixed chair. "I hate chairs that are stuck to the ground. What's it about, anyway? Is there some mad thief targeting all the fast-food joints in the country, shoving crap plastic seats up his jumper and running off?"

Neither of us answered. We knew better.

"They're made for midgets. There's never enough room."

I stared at him. "How can you be on a break already? You've only been working twenty minutes."

He nodded his head in the direction of the kitchen. "Sue's on duty today," he said, stealing a chip from my tray. That was all the explanation we needed.

"I don't know what she sees in you," Casey told him, ripping open the plastic bag protecting his toy.

"The Edster's charm." He flashed a mouthful of white teeth.

"Man, she's old enough to be a granny," Casey protested.

"She is a granny, but not mine, so who cares? If she wants to give me special treatment from time to time, all I can say is, go Suz!"

We laughed.

"Speaking of grannies," Ed went on, glancing up at the clock. "Mum got a call from mine last night."

"What's up?" As Casey asked the question, he scrutinized the toy. "It's that character from that new kids' movie," he blurted, interrupting Ed's reply. He frowned at the purple pig. "What a con."

"Nothing's up, but Mum said she might go visit her next week," Ed replied, ignoring Casey's tantrum.

"You going?" Ed's gran lived about three hours north.

He shook his head. "No way. There's Rhona's party and remember I told you Bill O'Grady could be watching one of our games this month?"

"The talent scout?" Casey interrupted.

Ed nodded. "Some of the guys at the gym reckon he'll be

there this weekend or next so I don't want to be stuck up in Newcastle listening to Gran going on about the war when Bill O'Grady is just waiting to be impressed."

"Isn't your gran too young to remember the war?" Casey asked, biting the burger, then spitting out the pickle.

"Mate, it doesn't have to be any war in particular. Honestly, once she gets started on poor Aussie soldiers fighting overseas, you'd volunteer to be a suicide bomber just to escape."

Casey reached for the toy pig again and studied it closely. Ed snatched it from him in exasperation. "It's a water pistol!"

"Of course it is. Everything is these days." Casey grabbed it back. "Making a toy squirt water doesn't impress people any more. They're just too lazy to come up with something new."

"You should complain," I suggested, trying to keep my face straight.

Ed shifted in the hard chair. "It's a shame you didn't get here earlier, Casey."

"Why?"

"I just gave out a skateboard with the last Zigglet Meal before you came in. And see that kid over there?" He pointed to a little boy standing in the line. "He's getting a PlayStation. In fact, man ... and I'm going to be brutal here ... we keep all the junk for you."

Casey flicked an ice cube at him and missed.

"Hey," I said, as inspiration struck, "if Ed's at home alone, we can crash there after Rhona's party, can't we? We can tell our parents we're staying at Ed's and just not mention that your mum isn't going to be there."

"Good one," said Ed, reaching over for my drink. "Do you think your mum will go for it?"

"Probably. She's freaking out about *PINK* so that keeps her off my back."

"*PINK?* Is it 'colouring your life' Tommo?" mocked Casey, quoting the mag's dumb slogan.

Ed snorted Fanta through his nose.

"Personally, I think they should have called it *BRA*," I told them. "Then they could have used 'We'll Support You'!"

They laughed.

"Or what about *Giggle?*" said Casey. "'Once You Start, You Can't Stop'!"

"Or *Tampon*," said Ed. "'Stick...'"

"Edward!" Sue was pointing at the queue of schoolkids that had formed since we'd been talking.

"Hold that thought. The Edster is in demand," he said, jumping up, banging his knees on the table. He swore loudly as he left us.

"That's one thought I won't be holding," I said.

"I agree." Casey shuddered and piled all our rubbish up neatly on one tray. He made a face when he got some sauce on his hand and looked around frantically for a napkin. He's such a girl at times.

5

When I got home, there was a note on the kitchen bench.

Tommy,

Had to make life or death dash to the office. Back at 10-ish. Have leftovers for dinner.

Love You

M xxxx

I did. Leftover Thai always tastes good to me. Afterwards I made a start on my English homework. Mr Darcy's not the only one who can write a good letter.

I was just attempting the opening when my pen ran out. I scouted around my desk and my bag but I couldn't find another one that worked so I went to grab one from Mum's desk.

When she's on a deadline, Mum's study's a mess but it always smells great. She burns scented stuff. The room's painted white, but one wall is this brilliant red colour. The bookshelves reach the ceiling and are crammed. She's read everything several times. Typical chick.

Although she's messy, she's really fussy about how things

are positioned in the room. It's arranged according to the laws of Feng Shoe. Feng Shoe is a Greek theory about creating peace and harmony by moving your furniture around a lot. The last magazine that Mum edited was a home decor one and, as she was also working on a gossip mag at the same time, her stress levels went through the roof. She did a big clean out and feng shoed the house. Sometimes even Dad and me had to stay in certain positions when we were sitting in the living room. Can't say it's worked though. Maybe her wall is the wrong shade of red, or maybe all her careful design has been cancelled out because the room is never tidy. The rest of the house is always pristine, thanks to Jan, our cleaner. After Jan's been in on a Friday, Mum patrols the house like border control making sure we don't make too much mess before her next visit.

Jan has always been banned from Mum's study for obvious reasons. Tonight, for example, the floor was covered in girly gear: lipsticks, sachets of cream, nail varnish … was that a pink G-string? I was about to pick it up when the phone rang. Guiltily, I jumped back and sprang to her desk to answer it.

"It's me, Tommy. You OK?"

"Yes. You?"

"God, no! Our cover is just not working, I still haven't heard back from our agony aunt, my art director has the flu and the coffee machine has gone on strike."

"Yes… Mmm… Yes," I murmured at what I hoped were the appropriate times, while fingering some papers on her desktop: blank paper but not the cheap stuff. I leaned back in her high-tech chair. It was better than a carnival ride.

"Anyway, I'll be a little late. Don't wait up ... lock up before you go to bed ... and Tommy ... I hope you're not swinging on my chair?"

I straightened.

"I'm presuming that you *are* snooping around in my study?"

"I was only looking for a pen," I protested.

"Just as long as you're not trying on the make-up ... or the G-string."

"MUM!"

"Has your father called tonight?" she asked, changing the subject.

"Not yet, was he supposed to?"

"No, not especially, but he usually checks in with us most days."

I thought I detected just a hint of loneliness in her voice. Great. That was all she needed when she was on deadline.

"He'll probably call you on your mobile." Even before she shrieked with laughter, I realized my mistake. Dad's great but he's the biggest tight arse at times. I swear he'd recycle toilet paper if he could get away with it.

"I'll tell him he can get you at your office," I offered.

"He can't. The switchboard is closed and you know your father, he'll never remember the number for my direct line."

"I'll pass it on when he calls."

She brightened and after her usual, "Goodnight, I'll try not to wake you when I get in," she was gone.

I checked out her paper again. It felt crisp in my hands.

She wouldn't mind if I borrowed a few sheets for my assignment. Amy Jones looked like a quality paper kind of chick. I gathered it up and grabbed a pen from the vast collection on Mum's desk, nudging the keyboard of her computer as I did, waking it up from its well-earned sleep. It glared at me. Bet it didn't have this attitude with Mum.

A sent email was still on the screen. I didn't mean to read it – but you know how it is when you just happen to catch sight of your own name.

It was addressed to one of her colleagues at the magazine.

"Blah, blah, blah … *but take my Tommy. He's a perfect example of the kind of boys that our readers are obsessing over. I might be biased, Lydia, but he's handsome, sporty, fairly smart when he tries and he has a good sense of humour…*"

God, she was embarrassing me. I was all of the above, although her "when he tries" comment was a bit harsh. I read on to discover what else she loved about me.

" *… but he has <u>no clue about women</u>.*"

I gasped. She'd even resorted to underlining.

"*Take last year, for example: he was seeing this little girl in his class and he tortured himself for weeks about what to get her on Valentine's Day. I told him he couldn't go wrong with flowers and chocolates. In the end he left it to the last minute, went to the service station down the road and bought her a plastic rose and a Kinder Surprise egg!!!*"

What? Sonia Hommes loved that present. Too bad she had to get rid of it because of her weird allergies to dairy and plastic. I read on.

"*Believe me, if our readers are trying to train today's teenage boys to be tomorrow's prime catches, they need all the help* PINK *can give them.*

"*I'm going to run with Carrie Edwards's advice column despite Marcie's objections about it being clichéd, and while I love Mark's title, 'Boofhead Busters' (v. funny) we can't use it. We don't want to insult our male demographic who will definitely read* PINK *when they're supposedly teasing some girl about reading it but avidly scanning every word.*"

I couldn't believe it. What was with women this week? First, Amy Jones and the coven of witches in my English class were having a go, and now my own mother was at it too. I sent the computer back to sleep and left the room in disgust.

By the time I sat down at my own desk to write my kick-arse letter to Amy, I felt too edgy to do anything. I abandoned it. And it was definitely NOT because I didn't know what to write! I had an early night.

Mum didn't wake me when she got home. Something else did.

6

A mobile phone ringing in the middle of the night is a very brutal sound.

Startled, I bolted upright in bed, my body acting without my brain's permission. An intermittent white light glowed eerily to my left. I reached towards it instinctively, knocking over the glass of water that sat there. I didn't have to see it to know that the spreading puddle was about to do some serious damage.

"Shit!" I moved quickly to save my phone from the flood. It vibrated in my hand. I stole a quick glance at the time. 1.35 a.m.? I fumbled to answer it. Was it Mum? Why wasn't she home? Had something happened?

"Yeah?" I said fearfully, my voice thick with sleep.

"Tommo? It's me." A hiss.

"Who?"

"Me!"

Suddenly, I was wide awake.

"Casey? Is that you? Where are you? What's going on?"

"Tommo, there's all sorts of crap going down here tonight."
He sounded far away.

"Down where? What's up, Casey? Where are you?"

"At home … in my room … I'm whispering," he added unnecessarily.

"Are you OK?" I found myself whispering too.

"No. Well, I suppose so… It's just that everyone else has finally lost it."

Lost it? That was hard to believe. The Caseys never lost anything, least of all their cool.

"Go on," I urged, propping myself up on my pillows feeling relieved. Mum must be safely tucked up in bed.

He took a deep breath. "It's Mikey … he's come out!"

"Out where?" I murmured.

"OUT!"

I may have gasped a little, but then I definitely remained speechless. If Casey's older brother Mikey had been in a coma or even in the army, this would have been really good news … but he wasn't!

"*Closet* out?" I asked finally.

"Yes," he snapped.

More silence. There was no way I was speaking first.

"Dad went mental."

I couldn't even begin to imagine it. Casey's old man is straighter than straight. He does everything by the book. He works in the Tax Office, for God's sake. Tax Office workers don't go mental. Everyone knows that postal workers have that covered.

"Did you have any ... I mean ... did you suspect anything?" I asked.

"Did you?"

"You're his brother, mate." I stalled.

"Yeah, but did you, Tommo? Did he seem ... you know? Was he ever...? Ah, shit!" He broke off, his voice full of despair.

I struggled for something to say to make him feel better.

"I've never actually thought about it, which is a good thing really, because it means he's not an obvious..." I stopped, unsure about how to finish my sentence. Fag? Queer? Gay? Homo? Insults we threw so easily at each other every day suddenly felt like lead weights in my mouth.

Had I suspected Mikey Casey was gay? NO, definitely not. I'd never really thought about Mikey Casey that much. He was five years older than us for a start. He moved away from home when he went to uni and he works in the city somewhere. I don't even know what he does. But he's a good bloke. He gets our grog from the bottle shop if he's around on the weekend.

Casey interrupted my thoughts. "Go on, say what you were going to say, Tommo. FAG." He sounded like he was almost in tears.

I squirmed in my sheets. I didn't want to deal with this. It wasn't my problem. Should I cut him off and pretend later that my battery had died? My finger hovered over the button.

"What am I going to do?" Casey asked.

"What do you mean, do? There's nothing you can do, mate, except pretend it hasn't happened or, actually, we could always beat the crap out of him. Ed will go for that."

"DON'T TELL ED!" He was yelling at me. "Tommo, you better fu—"

"Cool it, I won't." I silenced him hurriedly. "It was a joke, Casey."

Not even the hint of a smile from the other end of the phone. I didn't know how to handle this new frantic Casey. Blokes don't make calls in the middle of the night. We don't have emergencies that can't wait till lunch.

"Have you called Lena yet?" I asked. Girls were good at this kind of stuff. Lena would know what to say to him, for sure.

"NO WAY!"

Back to yelling at me again.

"Mikey's a selfish bastard, Tommo. How could he do this to me? My life's ruined. I want to kill him." He spat the words into my ears with such force that I was shocked. He didn't sound anything like Casey. He was being ridiculous. As if his life was going to be ruined just because his brother was gay. Talk about overreacting. I was about to say as much when something stopped me. For the first time ever I had to think about what I said to Casey. It felt weird.

"Look ... he's still your brother, right? You've always got on well. He's still the guy who slips you a twenty. He's still the bloke who gets us what we need at the bottle shop ... yeah? Know what I'm saying?"

Screeching silence. Apparently not.

"Oh, right, Tommo, as long as my brother is still getting us grog, I'll just forget tonight, will I?" Casey exploded. "I mean, as long as he's a useful fag!"

That word again.

"Casey, you're missing the point. I'm trying to say that … you know … he's still Mikey. OK, some people might not think of him in the same way now, but to you, he's still … well … he's still your brother."

"Yeah, but what is he to you, Tommo, and to anyone else who finds out? That's what worries me. I'll be the poofter's brother and everyone will start to wonder if I'm the same."

I just wanted to go back to sleep but I couldn't let this go.

"Mate, that's the most illogical thing I've ever heard. Are you for real? It's not like Mikey's contagious."

"Yeah? You try telling my dad that. And you watch, once the word gets out, I know people are going to look at me too."

Did he have a point? Of course he didn't. How stupid was that? But suddenly I was assaulted by the memory of Casey in Ziggy's, always fussing about the rubbish. That was a bit gay.

I yawned. "Well, no one else needs to find out, do they? We can keep it between the three of us."

"DO NOT TELL ED!"

"Hey, settle, mate."

"I'll tell Ed myself … later, right?"

"Right."

But it didn't feel right. I let it slide, thinking I'd raise the subject later when he was back to his old self. There wasn't much more to say.

"Can I get back to sleep now?" I asked, trying to break the tension. "I was just having a hot dream about your girl-friend."

"Yeah," he said, seeming reluctant to let me go.

I made an effort to reassure him. "Casey, it won't seem so bad once you've got used to it."

"Yeah, sure. Next week I'll get an 'I'M WITH FAG' T-shirt made for our brotherly outings up Gay Lane."

"Casey, an 'I'M WITH STUPID' one will do. Just wear it when you look in a mirror."

At that moment something seemed to shift, like we'd both watched a tightrope-walker plummet, only to land in a safety net that we hadn't known was there. He let out a huge hiss.

"So I'll see you in the morning, then?"

"Yeah." He hung on. "Tommo, we won't get past this."

"Of course we will."

"I don't mean us."

Who did he mean? Before I could ask he cut the line. *Thank God.*

Next time my mobile rings in the middle of the night, I swear I'm not answering it.

7

In the morning I found Mum in the kitchen engulfed by pink feathers, frowning at an empty orange juice carton.

"Why are we out of juice, Tommy?"

"New robe? Looks good." Sucking up usually works.

"Vera Wang … and I bet she never runs out of orange juice." She was not amused.

"Sorry, Mum."

"You put the empty carton back in the fridge. That's not only lazy, it's disgusting!"

I shrugged. She'd get over it.

"Seriously, Tommy, women detest men who are…" she searched for her words "… rubbish-challenged. You can see when something is empty and you definitely know where the bin is. Is it really too much to expect you to take the next step?"

I hate it when she's in this kind of mood. Before I could get a word in, she continued, "Women like men who take care of the rubbish."

"Well, I guess I'll never make a woman happy then," I said, remembering I was still angry about her email to Lydia. "But you already think that, don't you?"

I had her full attention now. *You goose, what have you done? Quick, back-pedal! Back-pedal! Don't tell her you read her email!*

I didn't have to; she caught on at once. "I thought I'd raised you to respect people's privacy, Tommy."

"Apparently not."

She bristled. "My correspondence in my study is off limits, you know that."

"I only went in to borrow a pen."

"And came out having read my private email?" She blew so hard on her coffee it spilled over the edge of her cup.

"Well, if you're going to slag your son off to a stranger..." I left it hanging and waited on a furious retort.

"Oh, stop being so melodramatic. I was writing to Lydia; she's not a stranger. And let's face it, I only said that you and boys your age have a lot to learn about the world of females."

"Well, you're wrong."

"Really? Enlighten me then."

"OK, maybe older women like you are a bit more compli-cated..." I stopped because she seemed to have frozen. I could have taken the comment about her age back but I decided not to. Served her right. I ducked her daggers and continued, "But today's girls want guys to tell them they look good and listen to all their boring stuff and that's about it. I can do that just as well as the next guy." I slurped the last of my cereal.

She took a long sip from her cup and placed it carefully on the bench.

"Don't worry, I'll save every issue of *PINK* for you and the 'next guy' and you'll both be fine in the end."

Very funny! I jumped up from my seat and almost left without putting my cereal bowl in the dishwasher. I should have. That would have wiped the grin off her smug face.

"And stay out of my study," she called as I stomped out the door cursing all the up-themselves women I knew. Obviously, I was still swearing by the time I got to school.

I kept my eye out for Casey in the yard but he was nowhere to be seen. Normally a freak about being on time, he was uncharacteristically late to Maths.

"Page 87 – Trig." I edged my notebook towards him when he turned up so he could copy my answers to the first section, save him going to the back of the book like he usually does. He ignored me. Fine by me. I certainly wasn't going to be the first to mention the phone call.

Eventually, he slouched in his chair and, whether deliberately or not, he angled his body towards me. I felt the pressure to say something.

"You right?"

He still ignored me.

Biting back annoyance, I tried again. "Things any better this morning?"

Big mistake.

"Oh yeah, Tommo, Mikey called again and shouted 'Early April Fools, suckers!' and we all cracked up laughing. He's such a joker, my brother." His eyes flashed, daring me to respond.

"Maybe you got it all wrong when he told you he was gay last night. Maybe he meant 'funny' gay and he…"

His venomous look stopped further wisecracks. "And just so you've got the latest news from the pathetic Casey family, Dad's blaming Mum. They've been at it all night. It's ironic, they spend most of their lives oblivious to each other and when they finally do communicate, it's a huge argument; like fighting about it is going to make a difference."

His bitterness took me by surprise. Funny, I always thought his parents got on fine. I had lots of questions, but I opted for "Why's it your mum's fault?"

He rolled his eyes. "Dad reckons he wouldn't have a 'poofter' son if she'd given him a decent nickname. 'Mikey for Christ's sake. No wonder he's queer!' That's what he yelled at her when he left for work this morning."

"That's the dumbest thing I—"

"I know. I know," he groaned, "but he's just not talking a word of sense right now."

"What did your mum say?"

"She said, 'I'm not the one with the dodgy cousin, Graham.'"

"What does that mean?"

"It's obvious, isn't it? Uncle Dick must be one too."

I'm sorry to say that I've never outgrown the need to snigger at the name Dick. Pathetic, but true.

I was swallowing my laughter when he continued. "I never did like that guy. He's not my real uncle, you know, he's only one of Dad's cousins." He practically spat the words out.

"Isn't he the uncle that remembers your birthday every year and sends you cash at Christmas too?" My sarcasm was lost on him.

"Yeah, exactly." He looked triumphant, then said, "They're good with dates, you know." Seeing my confusion he added, "Gays, I mean. They remember stuff that only women think about."

The bell rang.

My mouth was in mutiny, as we packed our gear away. My brain was commanding my words to lie low but those guys were pumped. They ripped into him.

"Get a grip, Casey … and stop talking about Mikey and your uncle as if they're another species who don't—"

"What the hell would you know?" Casey reared up in his seat, nostrils flaring. "You don't have a clue what you're talking about. This isn't happening to you! You wouldn't be such a big Mikey fan if this was your bloody perfect family. You've got no idea what he's done to us."

"Hang on a minute, mate, you're the one who woke me up in the middle of the night whingeing down the phone. And just so we know, I'm not trying to stick up for Mikey. I reckon his timing is way off. He should have waited till you'd left school just to be sure that you wouldn't get paid out."

"Yeah, right … I'd like to see that. Just let one bastard try to pay me out and I'll…" he spluttered.

"Is something wrong here, boys?"

Mr McGuire, our Maths teacher, was behind us waiting for us to leave so he could lock the door. Casey kept his back turned while I answered. "No, Sir, everything's fine." I gave him my brightest smile.

He wasn't fooled. "There wouldn't be any talk of a fight happening after school that staff need to know about, would there?" He'd obviously caught the last bit of our conversation and jumped to conclusions. I think they're trained to do that at uni. I hurried to reassure him.

"No. Casey was just talking about ... er ... he was just talking about..."

"Footy, Sir. I was talking about our footy team." A smiling Casey turned to face Mr McGuire.

"That's right, you guys are in the same team, aren't you? Mr Spencer's Under Seventeens? He's been full of your success in the staffroom. We're all sick to death of listening to him," he joked. "You must be well in the running for the title?"

"We are, especially with Ed on board," I agreed. "Did you know the Bombers' development officer is doing the rounds of the Saturday college sides this month?"

"No, I didn't. Great news for Ed Saunders."

We agreed.

"Right then, let me know how it all turns out," he said, ushering us gently out of the room.

"McGuire's all right, isn't he?" I observed as we walked along the corridor. I was hopeful that our united front with the teacher meant a truce, but Casey didn't even bother to reply. Talk about blowing hot and cold. I tried again. "See you at Ziggy's, then?" We didn't have another class together that day.

He muttered an answer, which I didn't quite catch and

moved purposefully away, pulsating frustration from every pore.

There was no point in following him. I turned to leave and bumped straight into Ed.

"He looks like a guy who needs to get to a toilet fast," he said with a grin, nodding in Casey's direction.

Nah, he was a guy who needed to get away from us fast. I suddenly felt angry with Casey. It's not like I'd tricked him into telling me about Mikey. He was the one who'd involved me. And I'd tried to help him. It's not like I'd laughed in his face and said, "Sucked in, mate, your brother's a poof." It's not like I'd done that thing with the dead phone battery and cut him off. And I'd followed through again this morning. And what thanks did I get? None.

Obviously, Casey was determined to handle this by himself now. I bet he was wishing he hadn't told a soul. There was no way he'd tell Ed.

I fumed. Not only was I roped into Casey's problems and getting no appreciation but I was also being forced to hide stuff from Ed.

It was dumb. Why shouldn't Ed be told? He was our best mate, after all.

In an instant, I made a decision. Casey was pissed at me anyway, so I figured I had nothing to lose.

"Ed?"

"Yeah, mate?"

"Mikey Casey's a fag."

I regretted it immediately.

8

I steeled myself for Ed's big reaction, desperately trying to work out how to play it down. I'd broken my word to Casey and it made me feel sick. Plus he would kill me when he found out.

Ed seemed to freeze on the spot for a split-second then he laughed loudly. "What's he done? Hang on, don't tell me he's not getting our grog for Rhona's party?"

I hesitated. Had I just been given a way out?

"Um ... yeah ... that's it..." I muttered and slapped his back. "Mikey can't do it. He's working."

"He is a bloody fag," Ed agreed indignantly. "Have we got a plan B?"

He was walking in front of me now and thankfully he couldn't see the relief on my face. He stopped outside Room Four.

"There's always a plan B," I told him, stepping aside to let him enter the Commerce class before me.

He pushed past me with another laugh that I knew was about to be silenced by the Bagpipe Bitch.

"Edward Saunders. I hope you've got your homework?" The teacher's beady eyes fell on him, giving me the chance to slip past. Hopefully, my own homework crimes would now go unnoticed. Ed shrugged his answer as he approached her desk.

"Go to Mr Day's office, Edward," Mrs McKenzie ordered. Really, she was seething and trying not to show it, but her accent always got thicker when she was mad. "I'm not prepared to put up with such a lack of commitment at this level. Tell him ye can stay down there with him until yur ready to take more responsibility for yur learning."

She placed some exercise books down on her desk but the fake smile she threw at the rest of us looked more like a sneer. We all knew that she'd much rather be dipping them in quickset cement and using them to beat Ed about the head.

"Oops, there you go, Miss." Ed stooped to the floor to pick up one that had toppled off her pile, grinning at me wolfishly on his way up. He drew his fingers across his throat. He knew I'd set him up. Then he made a point of walking towards the door in his own good time. The class watched the unexpected entertainment cautiously. No one was going to give the Bagpipe Bitch an excuse to turn on them.

Mrs McKenzie thanked him through gritted teeth and stood tapping her foot until he finally left the room. A quick glance at the clock must have told her she'd wasted enough time, so she skipped the homework check and moved on, just as I'd figured she would. I was safe.

But there's no such thing as sanctuary in McKenzie's class.

Pretty soon she was losing her nut again. I made an effort to concentrate. She was talking about elastic curves or something. I didn't have a clue what she was thundering on about, but I reckoned that she'd made a good point to Ed about being more responsible for our learning so I decided to take her advice. I abandoned Commerce in favour of my English homework. I fumbled around in my bag under the table and finally my fingers settled on the thick writing paper that I'd stolen from Mum's desk. I whipped it out while McKenzie was drawing graphs on the board and I was just about to place it inside my folder when she pounced.

"Thomas Sweeney, come out here and show us what you did next." She held out a blue whiteboard marker. I stuffed the writing paper into the folder and pretended to consult my notes.

"Come on, Tom," she said, impatiently as I slowly scraped back my chair, wishing now that I had been sent to Mr Day's office with Ed.

"Er … I'm not sure I get elasticity curves, Miss. I wouldn't mind seeing another example first."

The skin around her eyes shifted dangerously, a pool of quicksand sucking up her irises until they seemed to disappear.

"We're going over the homework, Thomas, so unless you didn't complete it…?"

I smiled and said, "Yes, Miss, I definitely did it but I left out the parts where I got confused. I was hoping to see you about them later." Grabbing my folder, I strode to the board, accepting the marker from her as I passed. "I'll show you what I've got for this one, but I don't think it's quite right."

I opened my folder, trying to give the impression that, like a smug TV chef, I had "one I'd prepared earlier" in there. I concentrated on the graph that she'd half-drawn on the board and began to count silently. I figured she'd jump in at around twenty. I'd reached twenty-six when she finally said, "Can ye complete this Tom, or are we going to be here all lesson?"

"Actually, Miss, this is one that I couldn't do." I snapped the folder shut as she moved towards me. She rolled her eyes at the rest of the class then she snatched the marker and began to attack the whiteboard with a series of quick blue squeaks.

I stood behind her for a bit then, when I judged that I could retreat, headed back to my seat. Halfway up the room I stumbled slightly on one of those guerrilla schoolbags that pounces stealthily from under the cover of a desk. In an attempt to straighten up, I lost my grip on my folder and a white envelope fell out. I swooped to pick it up.

"So that's how it's done," said Miss McKenzie, turning from her graph and flourishing the marker at me. "What's in that envelope, Thomas?"

Everyone was staring at me now.

Buggered if I know, Miss.

I didn't actually say that. I squinted down at it again.

It was unopened and addressed to my mother.

"It's a letter … for my mother. It fell out of my folder. I was using her desk to do my Commerce homework last night and I must have gathered it up with my stuff."

"Put it away before I add another letter to yur mother's collection about yur lack of effort in my class."

When she finally set us some written work, the collective sigh of relief to be off the hook was barely audible, but it happened nonetheless. I went back to my original plan to make a start on the English homework. I covered the elasticity curves on my page with Mum's writing paper and I found myself thinking about more interesting curves: Amy Jones's.

Don't get me wrong, I wasn't suddenly into her or anything, but a bet's a bet. Casey reckoned I couldn't charm her with words but he had to be wrong. How hard could it be?

Impossible, actually. Especially when the Bagpipe Bitch has stifled all your creativity. I just couldn't make a start. I glanced again at the envelope addressed to Mum in a neat hand. There was something about it that made me uneasy. What if it contained vital news that Mum should have had and she'd somehow missed it? I was pretty certain she'd no idea what mail had ended up on her desk, or disappeared from it as the case may be – and she was so scatty at the moment with the launch of *PINK*.

Jeez, I hoped this wasn't bad news. She'd never cope.

The temptation to know what was in the letter was too much. Hell, if I could break a promise to Casey for the first time ever, I could definitely open up someone else's mail. It was turning out to be a "How Low Can You Go?" kind of day.

I slit the envelope and skimmed the contents, knowing I'd have to deal with the consequences later.

Dear ... going overseas ... unexpected opportunity ... can't accept freelance writing job ... sorry for short notice ... hope you find another agony aunt ... apologies ... inconvenience ... Carrie Edwards.

Some of Mum's whingeing from our last phone call came back to me. No wonder she was still waiting to hear from the agony aunt. I almost laughed out loud. Funny that the person who was supposed to solve the chick problems ended up causing a big one herself. Mum would go ballistic! My brain dribbled that thought up the field, took a shot and scored an own goal: Yes, Mum would go ballistic ... at me! I'd taken the envelope and opened it and delayed the news that she needed a new writer. Why the hell couldn't bloody Carrie Edwards have phoned? Or emailed? Who writes letters these days?

She probably hadn't wanted to speak to Mum in person. I don't blame her. The word "can't" is not in my mum's vocabulary unless it's being said after the word "you" and she's looking at me.

What to do next? I could just march in and fess up. That would be simpler in the short term, but Mum is a long-term kind of woman. Every time she misplaced anything at all in the next twenty years or so, I'd get the blame. I could just hear her now: "*Tommy ... have you been stealing things from my study again?*"

Worse than this, the understanding that we have about my bedroom being my space would be gone. Now when she was looking for something, she'd be checking out my bag and my desk just to make sure another "accidental lifting" hadn't happened. I was already on shaky ground after reading her email the other night. Owning up was not an option. I could just leave the envelope on her desk and hope that she would find it and think that she had only got as far as slitting it open. Yes, that would be the way to go, for sure.

But I still spent the rest of the day mulling it over. When the final bell sounded I decided to give Ziggy's a miss for once. Probably best to lie low around Ed after my homework stunt and I didn't want to bump into an angry Casey anytime soon. As I walked across the yard, someone caught up with me and thumped me on the back. I turned around secretly hoping it was one of the guys, but it was Lena. The smile died on my lips when I saw Amy Jones beside her, glaring at me.

Right back at ya!

"Hey, Tommo! Are you meeting Casey at Ziggy's?" Lena asked.

I shrugged. She didn't need to know my plans. I wondered if she knew about Mikey.

"Is everything OK with Casey?" she asked.

"Yeah."

"Only ... he just seems a bit weird today." She studied me closely, waiting on a reply that she wasn't going to get. Finally, she said, "Can you give him a message when you see him?"

I was about to make some excuse when Motor Mouth Jones butted in.

"You'd be better sending a carrier pigeon, Lena. It would

probably get there faster and Casey would have more chance understanding it."

I ignored her. Lena laughed, putting her hand on my arm. I felt a jolt of heat.

"No, I'm serious. Tom, can you please ask him to call me? His phone's been off all day. It's not like him. Tell him I'm worried."

"Right," I said, tearing my eyes away from her.

Amy snorted in amusement. "Now concentrate, Tommo. Here's the message again: Call Lena. Phone – not on. Lena worried." She was using sign language and exaggerating every syllable through plump, promising lips. I had to remind myself she was taking the piss.

"What's your problem?" I snapped, letting her know I meant business.

"You," she said.

My mouth did its job and opened slightly to let my words out but the miserable cowards were taking cover behind my tonsils. Before I could muster the troops, she lobbed her parting shot: "Riveting as it always is to talk at you, Tommo, I have to go. Looking forward to hearing your Darcy letter being read out in class tomorrow though."

"They're anonymous. You won't know which one is mine," I snapped.

"Oh, yours will be the one written in Boofhead." That word again. She smirked and Lena smiled sympathetically as she allowed herself to be dragged away.

I made an effort to close my mouth. What were they going

on about, her and my own mother too? I'm definitely not a Boofhead. I am much more of a Mr Darcy. I can do the "sensitive male" thing with the best of them.

Take what happened last month at Skye Taylor's party when Emma Bates was really upset because Trent Wilson dumped her. Who sat with her for hours and listened to all her worries? Me! And I made her feel like I was really listening to her because I gave her deep eye contact. I even did that fake little punch to the shoulder with a big grin thing and told her to get over him because he didn't deserve her. OK, so she wasn't up for a quick pash in Skye's parents' bedroom when I asked her, but she did tell me I was a great listener.

I am. All it takes is a bit of sympathy. Ask the right questions and agree with everything. It's not difficult. Those problems in the chick magazines that the girls read to each other in class are always the same: weight, guys and ... that's it, come to think of it. Nothing else. How much of an expert do you need to be to understand women? Carrie Edwards would have been earning money for nothing if she'd done the job for Mum instead of sneaking off overseas.

Mum and Amy Witchface had it all wrong about me. Getting inside a chick's mind is not rocket science. I was going to write the best bloody Darcy letter ever in Austen English and there wouldn't be a single word of Boofhead to give me away. I'll enjoy the look on Amy's face when the best letter turns out to be mine and then I'll go right home and brag to Mum about it. Too easy. Pity I couldn't rub their noses in their feminist crap with something more...

An idea zinged in my brain. I checked it out from all angles the way you check out a zit. I hardly noticed I was heading home until I turned into my street. Now this was what I called a *Challenge*. It was bold. It was daring. *Could it be done?*

Yes, it could.

9

I don't understand how people survived without mobile phones. I called Ed first.

"Tommo, where the hell are you? I'm sitting here like a loser in Ziggy's waiting for you guys! And I'm going to kick your head in after that little homework stunt in Commerce. Is Casey with you?"

Oops, guess neither of us had told Ed that Ziggy's was off this afternoon. I stopped at my gate.

"Er ... something came up, mate. Stay put and I'll be there in fifteen."

"Hurry up then or I'll be forced to actually eat the food."

"Forced to pay for it before you eat it, you mean." Smiling, I hung up and hit the button for Casey's number.

"Yeah?"

His quick reply threw me. It felt like his phone hadn't even had time to ring.

"Yeah?" he repeated. "Tommo, is that you?"

Caller ID.

"Yeah." I listened hard for a clue to his mood. Was he "Cool Casey" or "Nutso Casey"? It was pretty difficult to tell at the moment.

"Whatsup?"

"Nothing much."

"You at Ziggy's with Ed?" he asked.

"Nah. Had something…"

"Me too."

"You busy?"

"Not really."

"Then get down to Ziggy's now. Ed's waiting for us. I'll meet you both there in fifteen. We've got work to do."

"What kind of work?"

"Mate, I have a plan. See you soon." I cut off his questions, feeling absurdly pleased with myself. We were cool again. Our friendship had stopped hiccupping and we hadn't even had to stand on our heads and drink a glass of water.

I stomped up the garden path but halted when assaulted by a humungous spider's web. I did that very uncool, manic arm-flaying thing and cursed Mum for insisting that we have a flowery bush-lined path leading to the front door.

"Mum?"

There was no reply. The door had been locked, but her car was still parked in the driveway, so perhaps she was around somewhere.

I knocked on her study door. No answer. I headed for the kitchen. There was a note on the table.

Tommy

Dashed back to the office with Lydia. Another bloody emergency with the cover proofs!!!!!!!! This mag is turning out to be a disaster!!!!!!!

If Dad calls, tell him it's all going fine. You know how he worries!!!!!!!

Study, please!!!

Don't wait up.

Mum

XXX

PS Order some takeaway from the pizza place. There's cash in the kitchen drawer.

PPS Don't get anything with olives ... you don't like them!!!!!

She was right about that. Olives are gross. I hate how they suck people into eating them because they look like grapes, but I think I would have remembered my aversion to them without a double PS from Mum. And how many exclamation marks can one note have? I felt harassed just reading it. Still, it did mean that the coast was clear for me to do some essential research for my plan. Despite her warning, I made a beeline for her study.

The rug was still soiled, a sure sign that she was snowed under, and something else was odd ... I sniffed the air ... she'd been smoking in here. This was terrible – she gave up five years ago. I spotted an overflowing plate on her desk next to her computer. I pushed the foul, makeshift ashtray away.

Five years of missed ciggies is a lot to catch up on but clearly she'd given it her best shot.

Disgusted, I booted up the computer. Just as I'd hoped, she hadn't taken her thumb drive with her. She's a religious file backer-upperer so she's always got several on the go. I connected the drive and entered Carrie Edwards's name in the search field. In a blink, a document named "Edwards Contract" appeared. I clicked to open it and was instantly rewarded with all the information I needed.

Mum had posted this contract to Carrie Edwards about a week ago, going by the date. All the details of their arrangement were included and, far from causing me any headaches, they made my job easier. I read through them a few times and committed them all to memory.

Our sex change was going to be a lot simpler than I'd anticipated.

10

Crossing Ziggy's parking lot, I could see Ed and Casey sitting at our regular table. Casey had seemed much more like his old self during our call, but you can never be sure with phones. Neither of us had volunteered proper explanations for the fact that we'd deviated from our Ziggy's routine. They weren't necessary. The problem just fixed itself.

Casey chucked a wrapped burger at me and grinned. As usual, Ed was stealing a few chips here and there. I slapped his fingers away as they snaked into my fries. "Mate, when are you going to get over this phobia?" I asked, dropping into my chair.

Casey said, "And don't think we haven't noticed how convenient it is for your wallet. You never spend a cent in here now, but you still seem to eat enough of our stuff to keep you going."

Ed made another attempt to snaffle a chip. "I can't help it if working here has put me off the food."

"But you're not really off it, are you? You're just off paying for it."

"Tommo, there are guys in that kitchen making your burgers who I wouldn't even let feed my fish."

Casey shrugged. "Plastic cheese, rubber patty, cardboard bun, how can you go wrong?"

I laughed but Ed's horror was mounting. "The pickle, man!"

"So what? Everyone chucks that away."

Ed stared at him. "Exactly! How many of those suckers do you think we need each week? There should be boxes of them in there, don't you think?"

Casey and I nodded.

"Well, there's not!" he finished, triumphantly.

He had our attention now.

"What do you mean?" I asked.

He lowered his voice. "Let's just say, we're talking 'recycling' ... but I can't tell you any more. Employer loyalty and all that. Just consider this as a bit of a heads-up." He took advantage of our confusion and stole another handful of fries from Casey.

"You're so full of bull, Ed," Casey spluttered as he tried to wrangle them back.

Eventually, when they stopped mucking around, Casey asked, "So what's this big plan, Tommo?" He was unwrapping his Zigglet toy as he spoke.

"It's a water pistol pig again," Ed sang gleefully as Casey swore and flicked it at him.

"How would you two like to be the answer to every chick's problem?"

Casey gave me his full attention. Ed looked blank.

I took the now crumpled Carrie Edwards letter from my jacket and smoothed it out on the table. Casey scanned it quickly.

"Who's Carrie Edwards?" Ed asked, sniffing. He always sniffs when he's unsure.

When I pointed to myself, Ed still didn't get it, but Casey did.

"No way, man. You'll never get away with it."

"Not me, Casey. We."

"Get away with what?" Ed asked, his attention caught by the arrival of two seriously hot girls. They didn't go to our school – Uglychicks College wouldn't let them in the door – but unlike Ed, I was too distracted to focus on them.

"Why would you want to do it? And how did you get this letter, anyway?" Casey questioned, ignoring Ed as he puffed out his chest and eyed the girls.

I explained.

"Just confess and tell her you're sorry and run. She'll still be able to get another writer, won't she?"

"Probably, but that's not going to be her first response when I tell her what I've done. Trust me, she'll crack it." I didn't bother mentioning that concern for Mum's sanity was only a small part of it. This was really about me seizing the opportunity to make a secret point to myself. I did know how to handle women. Amy and Mum could get stuffed.

"Who'll blow?" Ed had tuned in again. I could see why. Two guys had arrived to meet the good-looking chicks.

"So, let me get this right, Tommo ... you're going to become Carrie Edwards?" Casey asked.

"Who is Carrie Edwards?" Ed hissed.

"But how will we set it up without your mum knowing?" Casey asked.

"I've thought of that," I told him. "I got a look at the contract she gave this Carrie Edwards. And all the details were there."

"Who's Carrie Edwards?" Sniff.

"Wouldn't it just be better to tell her and then soften the blow by offering to take Carrie Edwards's place?"

"Are you mad, Casey? Do you really think Mum would agree to me writing for her precious magazine? I got a C for English last semester. She thinks I'm practically illiterate."

"What's that mean then?" Ed asked.

We ignored him.

"Look, the way I see it is that I'm doing her a good turn. We all are. She doesn't need stress; she needs a writer. She already thinks she has one. And she does ... right here."

"Quit ignoring me!"

We both turned to look at Ed. He was furious. "Who *is* Carrie Edwards?" In his frustration, he spluttered the last question, spraying me on the face. His saliva stuck to my chin. They both stared at it.

"See, *that's* the kind of thing you want a toy to do," Casey said casually. "Enough of this water pistol rubbish."

I started to laugh and Ed reached for my chin with a greasy burger wrapper, dripping in sauce. It was enough to make me go for my sleeve.

"So what are we doing?" Ed had stopped sniffing.

Casey explained before I had the chance to answer.

"You were snooping in her study?" Ed asked, horrified.

I nodded glumly.

Casey continued, "Tommo reckons we take Carrie Edwards's job instead."

"How?"

"The arrangement they have is that all the writing is going to be sent by email. Mum is going to send Carrie Edwards the problems on a Thursday and Carrie Edwards is supposed to send back the answers by Monday. When Mum sent the contract, she asked for an email address so that they could set this system up. Of course, she's still waiting on this because Carrie Edwards isn't going to do the job." I sipped my drink.

"How are we going to get Carrie Edwards's email address?" Ed asked.

Casey thumped him. "We're not, you stupid bastard. We use one of ours instead."

"Whose?"

"Yours, Ed. edwards@mailwatch.com is perfect because it's got the Edward thing in it. Mum will never suspect."

"Are you sure you shouldn't just tell her?" Ed asked again.

I was sure. This was something I was determined to do. When it was obvious they needed more convincing, I added, "If you've any doubts about how stressed she is, let me just say this … we're talking 'Year Nine Camp' stressed!"

Ed recoiled and Casey turned pale.

"Man, that was bad," Ed said.

I nodded.

"Wasn't she stressed out about some magazine then too?" Ed asked.

"Yes. A home decor magazine. She was working all sorts of weird hours. That's why she was the only parent home when they called for someone to pick us up."

"I still don't know why they had to call our parents," Casey said huffily.

Ed's eyes were wide at the memory. "Why, Tommy? Why, Tommy?" he said in mock horror, mimicking Mum. "I thought she was going to kill you when you said, 'It seemed funny at the time'."

Casey started to laugh. "Then she yelled, 'Sneaking out into fields after curfew to push over cows is never funny,' and you made it worse, Ed, by saying, 'Don't worry Mrs S, we were only keeping up the school tradition.' That was when she really lost it."

"Who did she push first?" I asked.

"Me, and it wasn't funny," said Ed. "The way she kept repeating the word 'tradition?' right before she shoved someone was scary. I reckon Mr O'Shea thought he was in for a push too."

We were all laughing now.

"And what about the drive back? Remember that Indian meditation crap on the CD? None of us had the balls to ask her to put the radio on. He raised his palms and closed his eyes. "Ommmmm. Happy place. Go to a happy place, ommmmm."

"So what do you think?" I asked after Ed had stopped omming. "Do we do the Carrie Edwards thing?"

"Yes," Ed said. "If she's that stressed, we'll do it."

"Do we get paid?" Casey asked.

"According to the file, Carrie Edwards was going to invoice the mag at the end of the first month. We can do that. We'll just get a post-office box for Carrie Edwards."

"Hey, we've got a post-office box," Ed said. "Mum got it after she kicked Dad out. She didn't want him sneaking back and going through our mail during the day when she was at work." He put his hand in his pocket and pulled out his key ring. He selected a long, narrow key and held it up. "Box 104. Or as Mum says, 'Box ten: four. Over and out, you bastard.' Good one, eh?" But Ed wasn't smiling. "She's talking about my dad," he added, unnecessarily.

It was the most I'd heard Ed say about his dad in years. I glanced at Casey who was studying his water pistol intently. Not knowing if Ed wanted me to comment or not, I took the key from him and asked, "Is it nearby?"

"At the post office next to the station. She didn't want one at our local post office in case he was spying on her. She figured if we got one near school, I could check it every couple of days. So I do. I've got the only key. It's too far for her to come."

"We could use that PO Box as the address for Carrie Edwards, I guess. With any luck, Mum will send the cheque there."

"Sweet." Ed grinned.

Casey shifted in his chair. "Your mum won't phone Carrie Edwards if she's got a problem with one of her answers, will she?"

"No way! Mum is an email woman. She hates talking business on the phone. I'm amazed she even tolerated the snail mail stuff from Carrie Edwards in the first place. Trust me, once we send an email, if there's a problem with Carrie Edwards, we'll know about it by email."

"I've got another question," Ed piped up. "What if the problems are too hard?"

I looked at Casey. He looked at me.

"Come on, Ed … how hard can they be? They're chicks' problems."

He still looked doubtful as he stood up. Casey offered him the rubbish tray.

"Guys, diets and fashion." I ticked them off on my fingers. "It won't get any harder than that."

"OK … when do we start?"

"How about now?" I said. "Let's go to your place and send *PINK* an email from Miss Carrie Edwards."

"Oi … that's *Ms* Carrie Edwards to you two," Ed said, ignoring the tray in Casey's hands. "And don't mess with me, I've got my period."

11

We headed straight for Ed's after we left Ziggy's. When we got there, Mrs Saunders was still at work. Ed let us in and led us to his room.

"Jeez, Ed," I managed to gasp. "It smells worse than usual in here."

"Does it?" He sniffed the air, before grudgingly opening a window.

"Right," Casey said, sitting at Ed's computer, fingers primed for typing. "Let's do this. Your mum's email address?"

"Charlie Sweeney at pan publications dot com."

"OK, what do we say?" Casey asked.

I'd already given it some thought.

"How about ... *Here is my email address as required. I look forward to receiving the first two 'responses'. My post-office box number is 104, blah ... blah ... blah. Signed, Carrie.*"

Casey nodded approvingly as his fingers flashed across the keyboard. Man, he was fast. "That sounds good. KISS."

"What?" Ed was lost.

"Keep It Simple, Stupid."

Ed shook his head. "Hey, don't call me stupid."

Casey and I laughed, recognizing a line from one of our all-time favourite movies.

"We should watch that again soon," Ed said. "Come to think of it, what if…?"

"I'm going to send it now, if you're absolutely sure?" Casey cut in, ending Ed's "what if" thought. A good job he did because once Ed gets started on a "what if", we're all dragged down the path to nowhere. Casey's finger hovered above the mouse, preparing to click.

Ed glanced at me. "And we're doing this because…"

I took a deep breath and instantly regretted it. Stale air filled my nostrils as I finished Ed's sentence. "I stuffed up by accidentally taking and opening Carrie Edwards's letter and my life will be over if Mum finds out."

And because I want to prove a point.

"Fair enough. Anyone want a beer?"

Casey and I refused. If we're going to a party we drink, but apart from that, neither of us bothers much, which puts us in the minority at our school. Most kids in our year never get tired of pouring alcohol down their throats. Both our parents would kill us if we did, but Ed's mum has some weird parenting ideas at times. I remember once asking Ed why his mum let him drink beer at home and he said, "She just figures she'd rather I drink at home and get used to it, so I don't go nuts and get *totally* wasted when I'm eighteen." He'd been totally wasted at sixteen when he answered my question.

71

When Ed returned with his beer, Casey said, "It will be good to read problems from people with even crappier lives than ours."

Before I could respond, Ed said, "I don't see why your life's so bad, Casey, even if you are stuck with Lena."

I wondered if Casey would tell Ed about Mikey now. It seemed like a good time.

Casey clicked the mouse and sent the email, right before he lunged at Ed and the two of them wrestled on the hardwood floor.

Obviously, Casey didn't think so.

"I'm heading off, guys." I edged my way round them and out of the room. "See you tomorrow." I think they acknowledged me, but I couldn't be sure.

Back home I spent the next hour chasing the sports on all the news bulletins. When the reporter reached the token part of his segment, going on about some women's cricket team, I searched for the remote. Women's cricket? Give me a break. They don't even wear skimpy uniforms to distract you from the boredom. I switched channels but there wasn't much on so I decided to start my English homework instead.

I must have stared at the page for twenty minutes before giving up. It was almost eight and all I had were a few rubbish lines. I was never going to get this homework done. It was time to call the guys for help.

"No worries. Just give me fifteen to take a shower. I just got back from the gym with Crazy," Ed wheezed.

I spoke to Casey next.

"Anything to get out of here," he muttered. "It's like a morgue. Dad's done everything but put his funeral suit on and Mum has bought in a cupboard full of choccy biscuits, in case we have 'visitors' when the word leaks out."

"What visitors?"

"Oh … family and stuff. Once Mum tells Aunty Kay everyone will know. It's only a matter of time before they're all round here to spear the guts out of the topic. Mum would die if she didn't have chocolate biscuits to force-feed them with tea. Anyway, I don't want to talk about it," he snapped, as if I'd been the one to bring it up. "I'll see you later."

Great. I wished I hadn't called him.

12

While I waited for them I flicked through my copy of *Pride and Prejudice*. It wasn't as bad as I thought. I skimmed a few descriptions of Mr Darcy and didn't see anything wrong with him. That Elizabeth chick was a bit too fussy if you ask me.

Casey arrived first. He threw himself on the sofa and let out an enormous sigh.

"That bad?" I asked.

"What do you think?" he scowled.

The silence was uncomfortable. I felt like he was expecting me to say something but I knew it had to be the right something. I gave it my best shot. "Try not to worry. Your parents will get used to it eventually. I mean, look how long they've been together. For sure they'll work through it. They love each other and it'll be fine in the end."

I didn't get a chance to feel pleased with my reassuring comments because Casey made a weird choking noise and shot me a contemptuous look.

"What?"

"You don't have a clue, do you? You've got no idea what my family is really like."

I was stunned. Of course I knew what his family was really like. I'd spent hours at his house over the years. I knew Mr and Mrs C as well as I knew my own parents.

"What are you going on about?"

He turned away and, just as I was certain that he'd shut me out again, he began to speak.

"Tommo, the happy Casey family is one big—"

"Hey, guys, The Edster has arrived!" Ed yelled from the hallway. The front door slammed behind him.

I took one look at Casey and knew that I wasn't going to hear any more. Instead, he fixed a smile on his face and greeted Ed as he came into the living room, then they both turned to me and waited expectantly.

"The letter's in my room," I said and when I got up, they followed. I plonked myself down at my desk, Ed took the bed and Casey sank into the armchair by the window.

"Feels weird writing by hand and not keyboard. I think that's why I got stuck and needed you two," I observed, waving the letter at them.

"Can't you type it?" Ed asked.

"Nah, Lennon said we have to handwrite it." I smoothed it out on the desk and began to write. "OK, how about this? Amy…"

"Nah, too boring," Casey said.

"My Dear Amy?"

"Too blah," Ed judged.

"Right … too 'blah'. That's top feedback, mate."

He smiled proudly. "How about … Madam?" he asked.

I looked at Casey. He was as surprised as me.

"Yeah, I like that. This is going to be easy."

We grinned.

"What next?" Ed asked.

I checked out my notes on the task. *Say something nice about the person you're writing to.* This would be harder.

A thought struck me. "Hey, Casey, who are you writing to? Have you done yours yet?"

He shook his head. "I'm going to cop the detention instead. Much easier than having to do it, but just to show you I'm prepared to pull my weight on someone else's task, I'll write the first part. Say something nice about her, right?"

We nodded and waited patiently as he began to dictate.

"Madam…"

I scribbled furiously.

"You have nice … tits." He flopped back in the chair, creased with laughter.

Ed agreed immediately. "They're like…" he groped the air desperately with clawed hands, "… a pair of jawbreakers, only much bigger." His eyes glazed over. "Hey, what if jawbreakers really did come that big? How long would they last?"

"I haven't had a jawbreaker in years," Casey mused. "Have you, Tommo?"

"Not since primary school. Anyway," I said, taking another shot at steering the conversation back, "the tits thing won't work."

"Even if we used another word for them like … bosoms?" Ed sniggered.

"Nope."

"Pity. That would've been funny."

I began again.

"Madam, I have kind of admired your…"

"Smart mouth," Casey said, suddenly. He looked at us. "Face it, you've got to admire how fast she burns people."

I nodded.

"Look what she did to Farnsy the other day," Casey continued.

I laughed.

"What did she say to Farnsy? Hope she got him good. I hate that prick." Ed stretched out on my bed.

"Well, Farnsy came into English last week with a necklace on, right?"

"No way! Like a chick's necklace?" Ed was incredulous.

"No, it was a pair of dog tags that he reckoned belonged to his dad, but they looked new. He probably bought them at that Concept store in the mall. The army look is in for guys right now." They stared at me. "What? Mum mentioned it."

"That's all bull, Tommo," Ed interrupted. "Guys shouldn't be into fashion like that. Oh, no offence, mate. I'm not talking about you. There's a difference between knowing a lot because of your mum's work, and being a homo about it."

I averted my gaze from Casey, aware that I was holding my breath. But Casey didn't flinch. It was like Ed hadn't said it.

I went on quickly, "Yeah … well anyway, I think he

thought he was going to start a bit of a trend."

"You couldn't miss them, either," Casey continued. "He'd even opened an extra button on his shirt."

Ed snorted. "What a wanker! I wish I'd seen him, I'd have ripped them off."

"Mate, no one needs you when Amy Jones is around," Casey told him.

"What did she do?"

"As she was walking to her desk at the start of class, he called out, 'Hey, Jonesy' and slapped her backside with his ruler," I told him.

Ed laughed. "Did she freak out?"

"I thought she would."

Casey agreed. "Me too, but she just turned and went to his desk. Then she leaned over him and flicked her hair."

"She's got nice hair," I said.

"Then she put her hand on the buttons of his shirt and sort of ran her fingers up his chest."

Ed sat up.

"Him and his dummy mate had nothing to say. Their tongues were hanging out." Casey laughed.

"So what then?"

"She sort of scooped the dog tags up in her fingernails and rubbed them between her hands."

"She's got nice hands," I said and took over the story. "By this time Farnsy was panting."

"So what did she say to him?"

"She pulled on the tags until his face was nearly in her shirt.

Then she said to his greasy head '*Dog* tags? How appropriate.' She threw them hard onto his chest and then she sauntered off to her seat. Didn't she, Casey?"

Ed was in awe. "You're right, that was much better than just yanking them off the loser and punching his head in."

We fell silent, enjoying the memory of Farnsy's humiliation.

I picked up the pen again: "Madam, I admire your smart mouth—"

Casey cut in, "But only when you are paying out someone other than me."

I nodded. This was sounding better.

"Maybe you should think about being nicer to people though and one day a guy might ask you out because..." He stopped and searched my face. Before I could answer he finished, "you've got nice tits."

We cracked up again.

"That is quite good, you know, mate," I told him when I stopped laughing. I wrote down most of what he'd said, replacing the last part with: "Because you're not half bad-looking." I read it out.

Casey raised his eyebrows. "Really? Is that what you think?"

"Come on, Tommo, she's a scary skank," Ed said. "I'm going for a pee."

As he left the room, scratching himself, I called, "Don't forget to put the seat back down. I mean, it's not like I can blame it on Dad this month."

I turned back to Casey. "What?"

He gave me a sly smile.

"What?" I said again and chucked a pillow at him.

"Oh, she's got nice hair … oh, she's got nice hands," he mimicked, waving his fingers in my face. "You've got the hots for her, haven't you?"

I considered that for a moment. The more I thought about her face, I knew it was true. OK, she was nothing spectacular … but her hair was brown with some really cool blond bits around her face and she usually wore it long and loose. Her eyes were a green twinkling colour, which sort of matched her hair, if you know what I'm saying. I mean they worked well together. All the bits of her face did … like they all knew their field positions and played them. Come to think of it, those guys could win an award for teamwork.

I sat up in my chair. Casey waited patiently for an answer, his eyes never wavering. What was going on? I tried to focus on thoughts of Amy's mean mouth. I swung the chair back and balanced against the wall.

Ed came back in. "What's up?" He'd caught the tension immediately. They were both looking at me now.

Think about the cruel words that snake out of those snide, curled lips, Tommo … those really, really pink lips … quite full lips, like she's done that thing the Hollywood actresses do and had them injected with pig fat, or whatever it is. Kissing them would be nice.

What had just happened here? One minute the joke had been on Amy Jones and now it was on me. Evil, mean, sarcastic Amy Jones was … hot. This was a disaster. I'd suddenly gone right off this task: it was time to finish and get the guys the hell out of here before Ed worked out what was going on too.

I sat upright again and quickly read our previous attempt. "We're just going to have to make it sound more Jane Austenish," I told them.

"You're on your own there, guys," Ed said. "We're doing Paul Jennings in our class."

I turned to Casey. "What do we actually want to tell her?"

I knew the stuff I'd just thought about her face would be good but I didn't want to give myself away, especially when I was trying to understand these new feelings. Anyway, she was up herself enough as it was. Imagine what she could do to me with this knowledge? It would be like giving her a weapon of mass destruction. She'd take me down in a nanosecond.

"We'll stick with the smart mouth stuff because it is actually the truth … and then maybe we could say something that told her she could be quite attractive, if she wanted to be?" Casey ventured, still looking bemused.

"Can we just be quick?" Ed said, yawning again.

"Yes, that'll work. Pass me the thesaurus, Casey. We need bigger words."

By the time we'd finished, Ed was already asleep.

"Read it now," Casey ordered.

"Madam, I have admired your wit from afar. No one can dismiss fools like you can. Your disdain for others is masterful."

It had taken us nearly fifteen minutes to find "disdain"

but that was because neither Casey nor I could spell it.

"One day, someone might come along who really likes this quality in the Fair Sex and you could be proposed to, so don't despair. You must find hope, Mr Darcy."

"Excellent, and it will look pretty good on your mum's notepaper. Use some fancy handwriting when you do the good copy."

When I'd finally finished, I took some time folding it into two evenly creased halves. Casey watched while Ed snored.

"What?" I demanded again, but he just touched the side of his nose with his finger and winked.

I thought of asking him about the stuff he'd been going to tell me before about his parents but I figured he wouldn't now and I didn't want to upset him again. He was in too good a mood. Instead, I said, "I don't like her that much." He grinned as he moved to my bed and gave Ed's arm a shake.

"Don't tell Ed," I warned.

"That makes us equal," he said.

Ed stirred.

"I guess it does." Two secrets from Ed.

"Did we finish?" Ed asked groggily.

I nodded.

"Phew ... it's hard work writing," he said, reaching for his jacket and heading for the door. Casey was behind him.

Once they'd gone I finished the assignment by writing the necessary names on the envelope, as instructed by Mrs Lennon, before stuffing it in my bag. I didn't want it to look too perfect or someone else might just work out that I cared.

13

Mum's car was already gone when I left the next day. Hopefully, she had made it home at some point last night. I sent her a text telling her to have a nice day. She replied at once: *Please refrain from subjecting me to ridiculous Americanisms. x*

I laughed.

I hooked up with Ed as he was leaving the train station and we walked the rest of the way together.

"So, what's the plan for the party next Saturday?" said Ed.

I shrugged.

"How are we going to get the grog?"

"I'll think of something, don't worry."

"We'll be right for some beer. One of the guys from the gym said he'll get us some for the usual fee."

"Who?" I asked.

"Marty Williamson. He works there and lets a few of the guys, like Crazy, train for free. He plays for the Bombers' Under Twenties. I've told you about him. You must know him, he's always in the paper."

I shook my head. "Doesn't the football club have its own gym?"

"Yeah, but it's for players only. There aren't any hot chicks there, either. You should hear the laugh they have with the girls who work out in Marty's gym. And the chicks love them because they're Bombers players. Ask Leens."

Hearing Ed talk about his gym mates made me uncomfortable. I'm not sure why, but I found myself changing the subject quickly. "Remember we need to check your email today – see if Mum's replied."

"Yep. I'm looking forward to it. I reckon I'm pretty good at this letter writing thing." I searched his face for irony but he was perfectly serious. "I'll log on in the computer room at lunch. Meet us there, eh?" he said. "We can probably send the answers back too."

"I doubt it. We'll need to think about them," I told him.

"Don't worry, Tommo, I'm a natural. And we'll be right if Casey gets his act together and actually helps this time instead of all that joking around about tits."

There's just no response to self-delusion.

The bell was already ringing when we reached the yard. "See you at lunch then," he said as he slouched off to first period.

I bounced up the stairs to English, two at a time. Casey was already seated. I plonked my bag down beside his.

"Have you seen Ed? Has he checked his mail yet?"

I glanced around the room. Amy had arrived but Mrs Lennon wasn't there.

"He wants us to meet him in the computer lab at lunch." I sat down.

"How's everything at home?"

He chose not to answer.

Mrs Lennon entered the room. "Right, people, homework first. Of course, some of you have handed it in early," Mrs Lennon said, beaming at some girls who sat up the front. She moved easily between the desks and gathered in the letters, smiling at some of them as she quickly scanned the quality. I held up mine, secretly glad that Casey had shut me down again. I was over him and his problems. I handed the teacher my homework. On returning to the front of the room, she held up her collection. "Right then, let's go."

We looked at her expectantly.

"Now, you were asked to select someone in the class and say something complimentary about them, à la Austen. I can see that most people have actually been the recipient of a letter, which is good. We haven't got time to read them all so I'll only read a selection and will mark them individually later."

She perched herself on the edge of her desk and pushed a strand of hair from her eye. For the briefest of moments, she looked as young as some of the girls in the class. The illusion was shattered, however, when she spoke again – her teacher sarcasm was pure adult.

"Anthony Farncinni, I've evidently misplaced yours. Just scout around the floor for me and see if you can find it."

Farnsy half-rose from his seat then thought the better of it.

"Sorry, Miss, I forgot to do it."

"Really? Then you can do it at lunch," she said in a voice so icy you could skate on her tongue. "And the others…" she looked slowly round the room. "You know who you are … Jack … Claire. I'll see you all at lunchtime in the library."

"Phew, I can't believe she hasn't noticed you didn't hand one in," I whispered to Casey.

He grinned.

"Tom, stop talking!"

I straightened up. Her eyes were slot machine windows. We watched intently as they spun. Farnsy won the jackpot. "This one, is in fact, for you … Anthony."

He puffed up his chest in anticipation. She began to read.

Don't know who thought Anthony was a "gentleman of means and graces" – she must be one serious nutter – but it wasn't half bad. Farnsy thought so too, judging from the goofy look on his face.

"And Tom, it would appear that you are our next lucky man to be complimented."

I blinked rapidly. I suppose I would have been cut if I hadn't received a letter, but now that I had, I was unbelievably nervous.

I swung back in my chair and tried to look cool. *Stop blinking … stop blinking … stop blinking!*

"Here we go." She began: "'Sir, permit me to tell you, you are one of the most modest, prettiest-behaved young men that I know, a fact with which you gladly counsel all. You are a gentleman of consequence, created by your own inventive fancy. Your Observer, with kind regards.'"

I looked frantically around the room for a sign. Who had written it? The words flashed in my mind: gentleman, modest, prettiest, inventive, fancy? Someone fancied me that was for sure.

My eyes bored into Amy's back willing her to turn around, but she didn't. Some of the girls were smiling at Mrs Lennon. Obviously, she knew who had written it. Her name would have been on the top. I watched to see if she looked at any one girl in particular, but she seemed to be sharing some joke with all of them. It was a bit of power trip for her when you think about it. I mean, at any stage, she had the potential to embarrass all of us by letting slip just who had written what.

I turned to Casey as casually as I could. "Pretty good, eh?" I got the words out disguised in a fake cough. People were looking at me. I smiled while waiting for Casey's response.

"You think?" he asked, after what seemed like ages.

I was about to reply, when Amy turned in her chair and looked directly at me. She was interested, I could tell. Pumped with confidence, I called down the room to her. "At least someone here's got taste."

Down the front, Dumb Carla giggled. Bet she didn't even know what she was laughing at, but then again, neither did I.

"So, you're happy with that, Tom?"

I prised my eyes away from Amy, prepared to answer Mrs Lennon.

"No ... you're not," Casey hissed to my left.

His comment threw me. I looked over at him but his eyes were fixed on the teacher.

I turned back to her. She was obviously waiting on my answer. Less sure of myself, I blinked a kind of morse code for "What the hell is going on here?" But no one helped. I considered my options and made a quick decision: avoid the question.

"Well, Miss, it could have been worse," I gambled.

She smiled, but looked unconvinced. "Indeed, it could have … I could have asked you what it actually meant, Tom."

Before I could work it out, she shuffled the letters again and, after selecting the next one, spoke to the class. "This one is for Amy."

I could tell from the paper that it was ours. I elbowed Casey but he'd already spotted it.

"'Madam, I have admired your wit from afar. No one can dismiss fools like you. Your disdain for others is masterful. One day, someone might come along who really likes this quality in the Fair Sex and you could be proposed to, so don't despair. You must find hope, Mr Darcy.'"

Everyone was looking at Amy Jones. I resisted the temptation to jump up and yell "mine!" I could still only see her back, but her shoulders looked like they were shaking. I felt a major sense of triumph.

"Look, we've reduced her to tears," I muttered to Casey, just before an enormous snort from Amy highlighted my mistake. She was laughing hard.

Mrs Lennon joined her. "So, Amy, what do you think of that?"

"Read it again, Miss."

She did.

I sat up in my chair. Something wasn't quite right about the way she was reading it. *Fools like you?* That didn't sound right. Too late, I realized I'd forgotten to include the word "can". It should have read "no one can dismiss fools like you *can*." It was supposed to be a compliment, for God's sake.

I nudged Casey. "I forgot the bloody *can* after fools."

"You don't say." He stopped to listen to Amy's reply.

"I imagine there's a backhanded compliment in there somewhere, Miss. It's good to know that I'm in my very own category of fools."

It was all Lennon's fault. She didn't have to read it exactly as I had written it. As if she couldn't see there was a word missing by mistake. She's meant to be an English teacher! I watched her chuckling with Amy. It's outrageous when teachers have fun at kids' expense. It goes against the laws of the classroom. I felt like lobbing a spitball at Mrs Lennon just to redress the balance. I shot Casey an exasperated glance.

He shrugged.

"Amy, perhaps this one will please you more."

Amy flicked her hair back from her face as the teacher began to read. "Madam, I have admired your vibrant, spirited being from afar and I beg your indulgence for the briefest of moments while I express my ardent affection for you…"

I leaned in to Casey. "Friggin' hell, 'vibrant, spirited being'? Who wrote this crap? She'll never go for it."

"Shh." He wanted to hear the rest of it.

"… love that has come into being like a delicate butterfly,

cocooned blindly until that glorious moment of its birth, fluttering and faltering, then gaining the courage to soar…"

I scanned the room looking at the girls. Most of them were doing that googly-eyed thing.

"'The courage to *soar*'? Give me a break," I said under my breath, without looking at Casey. When he didn't answer I turned to him. He was taking in the room. My eyes followed his gaze and I saw what he did. Soaring! Mass soaring among the chicks. Who was the smooth bastard who'd written this?

"… grant me my most fervent wish – to have you glance my way."

There was a lot of glancing happening now. Who had written the letter?

"Well, Amy, was that more to your liking?"

Amy Jones was speechless. I never thought I'd see the day. Her face was pink and, a bit like that Elizabeth chick in the *Pride and Prejudice* DVD, her chest heaved under her tight blouse. Not that we could see enough of it. I reckon that's where Mr Darcy was better off. The women all wore those corset things that pushed everything up. Very tasty for Darcy, but on the other hand, he would never have been able to tell a girl that her tits looked nice. That's where we are so much luckier. Today guys can say whatever they want.

"So who wrote it?"

Casey looked as bewildered as me.

"Buggered if I know, Tommo. It sounds like a girl's written it to me. It's too poetic for a guy."

"Maybe it was a girl, Casey. Lezzo alert, mate." Then I

thought about Mikey ... who was definitely not a lezzo but I wished I'd been more careful before opening my mouth. If my tactlessness bothered him, he hid it well.

"Are you sure you didn't shaft Ed and me by getting your mum to write a second letter?" Casey joked, and then his face became serious. He'd remembered the bet. "We had money riding on this and there's no way you've won if your mum wrote it. That's cheating."

I was about to protest my innocence when I spotted Amy looking our way. She had a shy smile on her face. And I remembered our bet too. Casey said I couldn't make Amy Jones melt, but someone had. How were Casey and Amy to know that it hadn't been me?

"Hey, Casey, maybe I did write something better in the end all by myself."

"Maybe you've just lost your bet, buddy."

I grinned.

"There's no way it was you."

It would be fun to keep him guessing for a bit.

Amy was still looking our way. I winked at her. It would be a laugh to keep them both guessing.

14

"So, it seems there is a guy in here who knows his stuff, Jonesy," I whispered in her ear as we filed out of the room. Her hair brushed against my cheek. It smelt of flowers, maybe roses. I had to stop myself from doing an Ed and taking a good sniff.

She spun round.

"Yeah, one maybe," she conceded. "The girls thought we'd go out and celebrate that heartening statistic tonight, then we'll find him, lock him in a cage and take a crash course in cloning."

"Good luck with that, but I think he's one of a kind. Much too complex to clone and, anyway, why would you want to share him when you could have him all to yourself? It's you he wants." I resisted the urge to laugh at her surprised face.

She was about to respond, but she stopped. Speechless. Twice in one day, it was a miracle. I decided not to push my luck. That mouth wouldn't stay closed for long and already I could see her starting to formulate a reply. I slipped away, joined the throng in the crowded corridor and went off in search of Ed.

The computer lab lived in the south corner of the school, along a narrow, dusty corridor. When we'd first started here, most kids didn't even know it existed and most of the teachers pretended it didn't. I guess it just meant a lot of retraining for them. Now it was one of the most popular rooms in the school. According to Mr Burrows, our principal, it's State of the Art, whatever that means. It's surprisingly light when you first enter and, as usual, I squinted when I crossed the threshold. Big, funky computers posed on the desktops. I guess they knew their powerful minds could solve every problem we threw at them. Although it was open to all students at lunchtime, it was the domain of the e-kid.

I glanced around for Ed but he was nowhere to be seen. Most of the students were in the zone, fingers flying over keyboards, listening to computer backchat through massive headphones.

Somewhere out of my vision, a computer yelled unexpectedly in the quiet room, like it had that condition that causes some people to shout stuff out at the worst times.

"YOU'VE GOT M—!"

"Shit!" The unmistakable sound of Ed, who definitely doesn't have a medical excuse, struggling with the volume.

I made my way to the far corner of the room. Ed's finger was tracing each word of his email across the monitor.

"Don't touch the screen!" I hissed in my best Baxter voice. Mr Baxter, the Computing teacher, went psycho if you touched the screens. He wandered round all lesson with Windex and a cloth.

"Friggin' hell, Tommo." Ed jumped, looking up. Then seeing I was alone, he asked, "Where's Casey?"

"Dunno. He said he'd be here." I shrugged, trying to ignore another surge of resentment towards Casey. He was so unreliable at the moment.

Ed was too excited to care. "The shark has taken the bait, Tommo!"

That's Ed for you, always thinking big. But Mum is much more of a shark than a fish, so I suppose he made sense.

"Shift over. Let's see." I squeezed into the seat beside him and we devoured the message on the screen.

> *To: edwards@mailwatch.com*
> *From: charliesweeney@panpublications.com*
> *Subject: Your Column*
>
> *Hi there, Carrie.*
>
> *Welcome to the team.*
>
> *Great to have an email address for you at last.*
>
> *Just a reminder that I'm proposing we work to the following schedule:*
>
> *• Copy from PINK mailed to you each Thursday*
>
> *• Return copy to PINK each Monday (4 p.m. deadline).*
>
> *I am certain with your Psychology degree and your experience in mags, it will all be plain sailing from here.*
>
> *Your first assignment is attached.*
>
> *Good luck, Darlink!*
>
> *Charlie*

"Darlink?" Ed raised his eyebrows. "Your mum can't spell?"

I ignored him. "Quick, let's see the attachment."

He clicked on the first icon, which turned out to be the contract.

Just then Casey arrived. "Sorry I'm late. I was with Lena."

We didn't bother to read the contract and opened the second attachment instead, scanning it quickly.

Dear Carrie,

I've been offered a place by two unis to study Commerce. One is just around the corner and the other is interstate. Naturally my parents expect me to stay at home with them while I study. They're both great but I really want to live my own life now. The interstate offer is not as good as the other one because there are some subjects that I won't be able to do. Should I accept it anyway?

Shaz (NSW)

Ed was the first to break the silence. "Let's read the second one. This one is boring."

I opened the other icon and we huddled together to read.

Dear Carrie,

My mother died of breast cancer three years ago and, while it was terrible for all of us, my little brother who was in Year Six at the time seemed to recover best of all. Now he's in Year Nine and suddenly he's in trouble at school and with the police. It's so unlike him. I know this is really about Mum. I've tried to get him to open up but he won't. Dad reckons he's just being a teenager. Sometimes I think I am the

only person who can see what's really going on with my family. Any
suggestions about what I can do to help him?
Britney (Vic)

Ed snorted in disgust. "I thought this was supposed to be a laugh, Tommo. Where's all the pervy stuff?"

"Buggered if I know." I turned to Casey who was oddly silent. "What's up with you?"

He shrugged but didn't comment.

Ed was still exasperated. "See, this is what I'm talking about." He didn't elaborate, clearly expecting that we understood.

"What?"

"Chicks and us. The big difference."

"What big difference?"

Ed looked at me as if I was the dumb one. "Chicks have to have a problem, Tommo, and if they don't, they just make one up anyway."

I was amazed at his insight. "You're right, Ed."

"I think Britney has a bit of a problem," Casey said.

Ed snorted. "Yeah, I'll tell you what her problem is – she doesn't listen to her old man, and don't get me started on Shazza. She must be mad if she wants to leave home when she doesn't have to. Imagine having to pay rent and feed yourself and all that shit?" His phone rang.

As I laughed, I looked across at Casey and my breath caught in my throat. I can't remember ever seeing his face more clearly and yet I barely recognized it. He looked like he'd been sculpted out of concrete but, the odd thing was, his eyes were tossing around in their sockets. Eventually they anchored themselves on mine and fell still. He was obviously thinking about his family again, but surely their problems were the complete opposite of Britney's family? Her brother had dried up, while Mikey Casey was spouting confessions like the Trevi Fountain.

"What's up?" His gaze was hard and challenging.

I was too confused to take him on. "Nothing." I tried to resurrect my strangled laugh. I looked at Ed but he was talking on his mobile. I made an effort to lighten things up. "Ed's a natural at this problem-solving stuff, isn't he?"

"Yeah, if he can ever remember his password."

"He knew it today."

"You better ask him for it just in case he doesn't next time."

"Passwords are supposed to be confidential," I reminded him.

He sneered.

"Look what happened to that Grovner kid."

"What?" he asked.

"You know, that email that went from Luke Grovner's account to that new PE teacher guy, asking him to meet him behind the demountables for a 'good time'."

Casey laughed. "How do you know about that?"

"From that nosy tosser, Kieran Donnelly, who of course just happened to be there when they confronted Luke."

"Well, he's pretty suss, isn't he?"

"Who, Kieran?"

"Nah, Luke Grovner. He's got to be gay."

Was this a trap? I thought about Mikey and didn't know how to answer. Instead, I said, "The PE teacher definitely isn't. The word is he's got a hot blond girlfriend. Anyway, it didn't come from Luke. Someone busted into his account and did it as a joke."

"Is that why he was off for a whole week?"

"Was he? I never noticed," I told him.

"He needs to toughen up. It was only a joke."

I agreed.

Then Casey said, "What if we think about these problems and get back to each other later with possible answers? Hopefully next week's ones will be about sex."

"Fine," I said. To my left Ed was still talking into his phone but he was giving me the thumbs up. The bell went. After logging off we headed to afternoon classes, but as we did I had an uneasy feeling that Carrie Edwards was not going to be the fun time she'd promised.

Typical woman.

15

I found myself falling into step with Lena Hughes on the way out of school.

She smiled at me. "Hey, Tommo. Have you seen much of Casey today? I'm still worried about him."

I remembered I'd forgotten to pass on her last message. Amy Jones had been right: a pigeon would have been more reliable. Still, with luck, she wouldn't realize that I'd let her down. I certainly wasn't about to bring it up.

"How was he at lunch?" I asked.

She looked puzzled. "Lunch? Wasn't he with you?"

"Yeah ... er ... he was. Actually, we were all in the computer lab working on something."

"Well? Was he OK?"

"Good. Fine. The same old Casey."

She seemed relieved. "Maybe it's my imagination then, but he just seems more distant."

"I'm sure everything's good, Lena. I wouldn't worry about it if I were you." But I was worried. Casey was lying to her and to us. I distinctly remembered him telling us he was late because he'd been with Lena. What was going on?

"Are you off to Ziggy's now?" She blew her dark fringe out of her eyes with a pout, which made her look pretty cute.

"Actually, no." I made a sudden decision. "Do you want to get a milkshake at the cafe?"

"Sure, as long as it's made with skimmed milk." She seemed pleased.

As we headed away from Ziggy's, I was glad not to be going there. I didn't feel like confronting Casey just yet and Ed was working, so unless Sue was on duty, chances were that he wouldn't even get out for a break.

And I had another reason for preferring to spend time with Lena. I wanted to pick her brain – research for Carrie Edwards's column.

"I'll get these," I told her as we went to pay for our milkshakes.

"Are you sure? Thanks, Tom. I'll get them next time." She smiled at me. I liked the idea of a next time. I steered her to a seat in the corner and we sat down.

Silence.

It was a shift in boundaries. Neither of us had been together outside of school without Casey, so I guess that's what made it so awkward all of a sudden. She kept her eyes glued on the table as she sucked on the candy-striped straw. Just as I was struggling for an opening line, she made the biggest burping sound I've ever heard. Not even Ed could have topped it.

"God! Sorry." Her face was pink and she almost jumped to her feet. For a moment I thought she was going to make a run for it.

I raised my eyebrows. "Excellent effort, Lena. I'm saving mine up for the end and I bet I'll beat you." I nodded my approval.

She flashed me a grateful smile and dropped back into her seat.

"How embarrassing." She covered her face with her hand. It was a very small hand. Delicate. Her nose was tiny too. It popped out between her fingers like a raisin, and I had a sudden urge to plant a kiss on it.

"Forget it, mate. Ed is a hundred times louder," I said, trying desperately to convince myself that she was one of the guys. It worked. Remembering she was Casey's girlfriend sure as hell hadn't.

She smiled again and took another sip from her drink.

"Can I ask you something, Lena?"

"Mmm."

"If your brother was getting into trouble and everyone else was ignoring it, what would you do?"

"You don't have a brother, Tommo."

Why couldn't she just answer the question? She was staring at me, making me feel like she knew the real reason I was asking. Should I just confess right now?

I pulled myself together. "No, but I've got this cousin, Britney, and she and I are pretty tight." I paused to check that she was falling for the story. "Anyway, we were at a family thing last week and she confided in me that her brother, Todd, is off the wall at the moment, getting into trouble at school and everything." I did a quick check to see if I was getting away with it. "And with the police too," I added for good measure.

Her eyes widened. "God, how old is he?"

"Fifteen. Anyway he won't tell her or her dad about what's really going on so she asked for my advice."

"What about her mum?"

"She died a couple of years ago from breast cancer."

Lena leaned over and touched my hand. "Oh, Tommo, that's awful. Was she your mum's sister or your dad's?"

Man, it was like the being in front of Burrows. What was with all the questions? She smiled encouragingly at me, looking genuinely interested.

"Mum's." Her hand tightened on mine. I liked it there. "She was pretty cut up about it. We all were." I looked slightly beyond her shoulder and concentrated on a faraway grieving look.

I must have nailed it because she squeezed again and asked, "Were you close to her?"

I nodded like it was too painful to talk about. We fell into a silence. If I didn't break it soon, I'd never get her advice. I gave a little cough to indicate that I was back in control then I shifted in my seat. "Anyway, I was just wondering if you had any ideas."

"Well, if she really isn't getting any help from your uncle and Todd is refusing to open up, maybe Britney should make an appointment with her school counsellor and see if there are any teachers who can help. Even if Todd doesn't trust them, they might be able to convince her dad that he needs to take Todd's issues seriously."

Pretty good.

"Does that help?" Her cute nose crinkled and I wanted to kiss her. More than I wanted to kiss Amy? Mmm. I couldn't decide.

"Yes, it does and I'm sure Brit will act on it."

"It must be really nice having a cousin your own age, especially as you don't have any brothers or sisters." She drained the last of her milkshake and sighed. "And I think it's lovely that she can confide in you like this. You must be pretty special to her. I wish I had a cousin like you."

"Hey, you've got Casey," I joked, trying to divert her attention away from bogus Brit.

"Yeah ... right! Casey is just like your cousin's brother. He's locked up tighter than a safe most of the time." Seeing my frown she hurried to explain. "Don't get me wrong, I love him to bits, but he can be really hard to talk to. Some days he just retreats to his own corner of the earth and it's really difficult to have a conversation with him when he's like that. He can be so secretive, you know."

I was stunned. Fair enough, he could be a bit intense when he was down, like he was at the moment with the news about Mikey, but Casey was still an open book to me and Ed. Well, maybe not to Ed right now but that was understandable. I thought back to his lies at lunchtime and squirmed.

"Anyway, back to your cousin," Lena said quickly. I'd taken so long to comment on Casey that she probably thought I didn't want to discuss him.

"I do think it's important that someone is looking out for her too. She can't shoulder all the responsibility. Perhaps you should mention this to your mum and maybe she can support her. I expect they've become close since her mum died?"

"Yeah. You're a genius, Lena!"

She looked pleased as she glanced at her watch. "I've got to make a move. Thanks for the drink. If Britney is ever round this way, I'd love to meet her."

I nodded and escorted her to the door.

So would I.

16

Saturday mornings were invented for footy. Mum came into my room as I was packing my bag. She was wrapped in a dead animal of some kind, dressed for the cold.

"Tommy, how long will you be gone today?"

"I'll be back this afternoon. The usual time, I reckon. Why?"

"Oh, no reason. It's just that I have to stay at the office and your father said he might call here around two. If I miss him again, we're headed for the divorce courts."

"Can't he call your mobile just this once?"

She guffawed. "If only Old Scrooge would."

"That reminds me, did you turn the heater off in your ensuite?" I asked. Our energy bills are probably the only thing my parents argue about. They've got one of those ceiling fan, light combo heaters in their bathroom. Mum switches it on all year round because she reckons it's got the best light for putting on her make-up.

Guilt sprinted across her face. "God, you sound just like

him." She rolled her eyes theatrically. "Be a sweetheart and do it for me before you leave?"

I nodded. "I'll tell Dad to call you at the office if you're not back."

"Good. Now, are you going to a party tonight? Because we need to talk rules if you are."

"No, that's next week."

"Right. Well, grab a pizza for dinner if I'm late."

"And if you're home?" I was hopeful.

"We'll grab a pizza together, but I'll pay!"

I chucked a smelly sock at her.

She squealed and disappeared in a flurry of perfume and fur. I wondered briefly if it was fake; probably not. Mum likes to think of herself as a major greenie but she never mixes politics with fashion.

She hadn't been gone long when Casey turned up at the front door.

"You ready?" he asked without coming inside.

I grabbed the key, slung my bag over my shoulder and closed the door behind me. Once again neither of us mentioned the fact that our usual after-school Ziggy's meeting had not taken place the day before. I thought about offering some sort of explanation but I didn't quite know what to say. For some reason I had the guilts about meeting Lena, but it's not like I was trying to crack onto her or anything. She's my best mate's girlfriend! I ignored the voice reminding me about wanting to kiss her.

"Did Ed call you?" Casey asked, suddenly.

"He could have. My battery's dead."

"So, you don't know then?"

"Know what?"

"Bill O'Grady's going to be there."

"Bullshit!"

Casey nodded. "Ed's sweating. If O'Grady picks anyone, it will be him or Kyle Rogan."

"Nah, Rogan's rubbish."

"He's good when he's on form, Tommo."

"Yeah, but Ed's always on form, isn't he? He's like a machine when he's out there. Everyone knows that."

"I wonder what's taken the Bombers so long to get their talent development officer round the local teams this year," Casey said. He was waiting patiently as I flayed madly at a spider's web that he had managed to avoid. I pulled myself together eventually, flicking the last of the stickiness off my face. Maybe because we were a college team they'd taken longer to check us out, but now that they were interested, I prayed Ed would catch their eye.

"How does he know the scout's definitely coming today?"

"That loser kid from the club called him – Randal Bedford, the one they call Crazy."

"Why do they call him that?" I interrupted.

Ignoring me because he probably didn't know the answer either, he continued, "He's in the Under Twenties and, according to Ed, he knows because he's tight with that Marty guy who's like King Shit of the Under Twenty side and knows everything."

"He's getting our grog next week."

"Is he?"

"So Ed reckons."

"I don't trust that guy," Casey said.

"Really?" I decided to confide in him. "Hey, does it bother you that Ed seems to be spending heaps of time with those guys now?"

He shot me a fierce look. "Why would it bother me?" He spat the words out, narrowing his eyes as he demanded an answer. "It's no big deal to me who Ed hangs with."

"I'm just saying that…"

"I don't care who Ed sees. I'm not his keeper."

I was shocked by the aggression. I didn't know what I'd done to push his buttons this time but no doubt it had something to do with him and Mikey again. I couldn't see how. Part of me wanted to laugh in his face at the randomness of his latest outburst and part of me wanted to kick his self-centred, stubborn head in.

Instead, I resigned myself to a new reality. This mate of mine could turn into a complete stranger in seconds. I started to explain what I was trying to say about Ed and his footy friends but I couldn't get the words out. I guess I couldn't concentrate on them because I was feeling so ripped off again. He'd just made me think I could talk about this kind of stuff and the minute I did, he made me feel dumb, so I gave up. He eyed me like I was a disappointing Ziggy's toy and walked away.

SO NOT FAIR! my brain was screaming, but who cared? At least I didn't say it out loud.

Anger surged and my bloodstream carried it, little bindies

of rage scratching through my veins and stinging viciously as they made contact with my guts. I was sick of letting him down and not ever knowing why. It was doing my head in that he couldn't be honest and say what was really giving him the shits.

As I followed behind, he suddenly stumbled. His shoulders stiffened when he found his balance but he didn't look back and I didn't guffaw or make one of those "Did you enjoy your trip, mate?" jokes. When I looked to see what he'd fallen over I realized it was his own feet. My resentment died. Another feeling grew. Pity? Sadness? It was unfamiliar. I only know I had the overpowering sense that I was losing something and there was nothing I could do about it.

So I didn't pour out all my other dumb fears about Ed. I didn't say another word about how I hated Ed having new mates who were better than us at footy. I decided not to tell him that I thought Ed should have been told Mikey's news too. There was no way I was going to tell him that nothing was the same now and we needed to sort it out.

Or maybe I should.

"Are you ready to go, or what?" Casey asked.

His words were a bucket of icy water on my face. I stared at him. Maybe the real Casey was trapped in there, desperate to get out. Should I take a gamble and tell him what I'd been thinking?

He broke the spell. "We're late."

I looked at my watch. He was right. We were out of there in seconds, but it was a long, conversation-free journey.

I saw the scout as soon as we reached the oval.

"There he is," I whispered to Casey.

"Why are you whispering?"

"I dunno." I laughed nervously. The truth was Bill O'Grady was the kind of guy that made you whisper. He was a scary old bastard. I stole another glance at him. He was rugged up against the cold with a Bombers beanie and a scarf worn over one of the club's slick new sports jackets. He was short and stocky, with spiked grey hair – an echidna with glasses – and just as prickly if all the stories were true. He was standing alone, so obviously no one wanted to find out.

There were a lot more people at the match than usual. The majority were crowded around Kyle Rogan. It looked like his whole extended family had turned up. In contrast, Ed was sitting alone at his spot under the jacaranda. He squinted up at us when we reached him and grinned, but he didn't stop stretching out his hamstrings.

"Did you hear, Tommo?"

"From *Casey*, mate."

"Hey, is it my fault your mobile wasn't switched on?"

"Casey and I have decided when we get picked by Bill O'Grady today, we'll put a good word in for you for next year," I told him.

He laughed. "Mate, the way you play, the water boy's got more chance than you have of being noticed by Old BOG." He held out his hand and I pulled him onto his feet.

"Is your mum here?" Casey asked, looking around.

"Nah, she had to work." He looked away quickly.

"Good luck out there, Ed." I slapped his back.

"I'm off for a quick warm-up run." He bolted.

"Right, Tommo, let's start our own warm-up," Casey said, chucking me a bottle of Coke. I took a few swigs and pulled off my jacket.

"That's me ready." I passed it back to him.

"Have I got time for a burger before the game starts?" He was eyeing the canteen in the corner.

"Doubt it. You'll just have to play on an empty stomach. If you get hungry, you can take a chomp out of their hooker. Plenty of meat on him."

We both looked in the direction of the players from St. Steven's College.

"Jesus, he can't be seventeen," Casey spluttered.

I knew what he meant. Almost every one of the opposition looked ten years older than us, and it seemed they'd spent all of those extra years in a gym. They were seriously buff.

I laced up my boots. "Guess we'll be dancing again."

"Definitely." He winked and I felt myself exhaling with relief. I'd survived his latest tsunami then: I could keep on treading water until next time.

"No way!" Ed appeared behind us. "You two are not dancing this game. We need hard tacklers. You'd better not run scared, Tommo. If you two pull any of those fag ballet moves, I'll kick your head in and I don't care if you are on my team."

I looked anxiously at Casey but, to my relief, he was laughing.

"Right, keep your hair on. We'll play hard, won't we, Tommo?"

I just didn't get it. How could Ed constantly put his foot in it with his gay references and get past Casey's new finer feelings about the subject, when I offended him by just getting up in the morning?

"You'd better," Ed said as we ran on.

17

We crawled off at full-time. Our heads were still intact but that was about all. The St. Steven's players were thugs. Catholic schoolboys always fought hard. It was all right for them; they could confess to ripping out a guy's lung in a sporting frenzy to a priest and get forgiven. The rest of us got to feel bad about it for the whole weekend.

We'd won the game by the slimmest margin, not helped by the fact that we'd lost our best player with twenty minutes to go. I looked over at Casey as he sat down on the grass. His nose was trickling blood.

"Ed's leg looked bad, eh?"

He nodded. "Broken, I reckon."

"Yeah, guess we better get to the hospital," I said, grabbing my gear.

Casey didn't answer.

"Aren't you coming?"

"Nah. Maybe later."

"Why not?"

"Got something else to do."

I scowled. Something else to do? "What?"

"Look, I said I'd see him later. How was I to know that he'd go and break a leg today? It's not like he's at death's door or anything," he snapped.

"Yeah, but he's just ruined his chances with the Bombers, hasn't he? He'll be feeling pretty sick about that."

He didn't answer me. He picked up his bag and turned to go. "Tell him I'll catch him later."

I was speechless.

The hospital was fairly new and the casualty ward was light and modern. As if that made people more comfortable to be there. It still gave me the creeps. I scanned the faces in the beds and saw Ed in the corner. His eyes were closed. I was expecting to see his leg stretched out in front of him in one of those pulley things but there was nothing. I stopped dead in my tracks. For a horrible moment I wondered if he still had a leg. Taking hold of myself, I approached his bed. As if sensing I was there, his eyes blinked opened, bright and laughing. Must be the painkillers.

"Hey, mate, how are you feeling?" I said in my best funereal voice.

"Friggin' awesome, mate."

Once the drugs wore off it would be a different story. "How's the leg?"

"It's fine."

I was surprised. "Is it broken?"

"Nah, I was lucky. It's just badly bruised and it hurts like hell."

I let out a relieved sigh. "So, you'll be back in the game in a few weeks, then?"

He nodded.

"Perhaps Bill O'Grady will come back and take another look. You were having a blinder before that guy stomped all over your leg." To my amazement, he laughed.

"Don't think he'll need to come back, Tommo. I've just accepted an invitation to go visit the club next week and sign a few papers. I'll be training with their Eighteens as soon as the swelling goes down."

"YES! Fan-bloody-tastic. This is huge, mate. When did you see Old BOG?"

"About an hour after I got here. He came to see how I was and made me the offer then. Didn't you notice he wasn't there at full-time?"

"Nup, I couldn't see a thing through the blood. Jeez, they were tough, weren't they?"

"Yeah, and they'll keep. Next time we'll be better prepared."

"So when are you getting out?"

"Tomorrow. Mum was in before. She thinks it's best. They're keeping me overnight because someone booted me in the head when I went down. You didn't see who, did ya?"

I shook my head.

"They want to observe me for twenty-four hours. Where's Casey?"

"He said he'd see you later," I told him.

Just then, a loud commotion woke up the rest of the quiet ward.

"EDDY!"

"GO THE EDSTER!"

"MATE!" A third voice rang out. Three guys were making their way noisily down the room. I looked questioningly at Ed.

"My Bombers buddies," he explained, before calling back loudly, "I friggin' did it guys. I'm in!"

They jogged the rest of the distance and high-fived him before noticing me.

"Hey guys, this is Tommo. From school."

I gave them a curt nod and glanced at my watch. "Actually, I've got to go. I'm expecting an international call," I announced, then immediately felt like a tosser. But the newcomers totally ignored me. I gave Ed a light punch on the arm and stood up.

"Thanks for coming, Tommo."

I turned back but he was already describing Bill O'Grady's visit.

I made my way out. *Tommo from school?* That's how Ed had introduced me to his new teammates. It made me sound like I was a kindy kid. I bet his new friends had known that the scout was watching today's game. I bet they hadn't been given the excuse they couldn't be reached because their mobiles were off. He'd have definitely tried their landlines.

I decided to call Casey and have a whinge. I also wanted to tell him Ed's great news. Perhaps it would make him feel bad that he hadn't made the effort to be there. If I was feeling lousy, there was no reason why he shouldn't be too.

His phone rang for ages before it was answered and when it was, the voice on the line wasn't Casey's. It was a chick.

"Hey, Lena?" I ventured. "Is Casey there?"

There was a seriously long pause before the reply. "Casey is busy right now. Can you call him back later?"

"Lena…?" Even as I spoke her name again I knew it wasn't her. "Sure. Who is this?" I asked, but the line was dead.

18

I was mateless on a Saturday afternoon. I couldn't believe it. It gave me the shits. I was wallowing in self-pity when the phone rang.

"Hi, Tommy. How was your game?"

It was Dad. "We won, but only just."

"It's the end result that counts, mate. Is Mum home?"

"Nah, she's back in the office again. Call her there on the number I gave you the other night. Don't go through the switchboard or you'll miss her."

"How's she bearing up?"

"Stressed to the max, but what's new?"

"Thought as much. Look, I'm going to be stuck here for another few days, mate."

Great! "She's not going to like that."

"I know."

"Is there a problem?"

"Yes, about fifty of them. This company must have put an ad in the *Idiot's Times* when they recruited their staff.

Honestly, I'm yet to meet a sane employee, let alone one who can actually locate the power switch on their computer without a map."

"That bad, eh?"

"That bad, but that's my problem. What's yours?"

"What do you mean?"

"Come on, I might be on the other side of the world but I can still tell when you're not yourself."

I didn't need an invitation to talk to Dad. "Ed got signed for the Bombers today."

"That's great news."

"Yeah, but he got hurt and ended up in hospital."

"Is he OK? Why aren't you and Casey there with him?"

"He's fine. It's just bruising and concussion. Casey wouldn't go to the hospital and I left when Ed's footy mates arrived."

"Why wouldn't Casey go?"

"He had something else on," I said sarcastically.

"Sounds like there's an issue there," Dad said.

"Things are just a bit weird right now. Ed's doing his footy thing and Casey's never around. It just feels different. I can't explain it…" I broke off.

"I don't know what's going on with Steve Casey but I suppose things will start changing now, whether you like it or not."

"I don't get you."

"In twelve months' time you'll be going your separate ways, despite your best intentions. I'm not saying you won't still see each other, but you'll have to make time to catch up and, unfortunately, other things will get in the way."

"Like what?"

"Like work or uni or, in Ed's case, footy. Then there will be girlfriends and new friends."

"So what? Everything changed when we started high school but we got through it."

Dad chuckled. "Of course you did. You were thirteen. Your problems were simple. Just learn to roll with the punches, mate, that's the best advice I can give you." He gave me a few seconds to let that sink in before saying, "Now let me off the phone so I can call your mother."

"OK. Thanks, Dad."

"You won't be thanking me when Mum gets the bad news about the change to my flight."

"Yeah, well, she's an adult. She's just going to have to roll with the punches too."

Dad roared with laughter. "Tommy, any advice I give you always comes with the qualifier: *does not apply to your mother.*"

"I'd rather it didn't apply to me and Ed and Casey."

He laughed again. "Hang in there, mate. We'll talk more when I'm home."

"Thanks, Dad."

Lena called a second later.

"Tommo, is Casey with you?" Something about her voice told me I should be covering for him but I needed more of a hint, so I stalled.

"He was."

"When? At footy?"

"Yeah … and for a bit after." I remained vague about times.

"Where is he now? He was supposed to come around to my place this afternoon."

"Not sure. He's probably on his way."

"Yeah. Probably. How did the game go?"

"It was brutal. Ed ended up in hospital but at least he impressed the talent scout. They've signed him up."

"Unreal. He must be pleased. Is Casey there with him?"

"I'm not sure … I … er … I left early to see Britney."

"How is she?"

"Good, yeah. Great advice the other day. Thanks, Lena."

"Well, I'm glad someone is interested in what I've got to say, because Casey isn't at the moment."

Not Casey again. I changed the subject. "Brit was telling me today that she's probably going to be able to get into two unis but doesn't know which one to choose." I went on to elaborate on Shaz's problem.

"I thought Britney was the same age as us?"

Shit, I forgot.

"Oh, she is, it's just that she is predicting that after next year she will make it into both places."

"Oh. Well, I think it will depend on how much she thinks her brother and her father still need her by then, won't it?"

Damn. That wasn't what I was looking for.

"I suppose, but what would you do?"

"I'd probably stay. She could still stay in the area and move out of home. That might be a good compromise."

Yes, that would work for Shaz. "I'll pass that on. Thanks for your help."

"No problem. And if Casey calls you, can you get him to call me?"

"Sure." I was reluctant to hang up but I couldn't think of anything else to say.

Later that day when I was bored out of my skull, Amy crept into my head. I reckon she suspected the good Darcy letter had been from me. I wondered what she'd do if I called her mobile. I could get her number off Leens, for sure. I thought about it for a second and definitely decided against it. Too chicken.

I spent the rest of the day watching DVDs but every now and again Dad's words appeared, pretending to be just sauntering past when really they were stalking me. I knew he was sort of right about just rolling with it but I wasn't ready to give up yet. I wanted to throw a few punches of my own.

19

I saw Ed first on Monday. He was hobbling gingerly along the corridor on his way to PE.

"Whatsup?" I asked, catching him.

He turned. "Nothing much. The leg's heaps better. It should be good by the weekend."

"You can't do PE today though, can you?"

"Nah, I have to sit out."

"Do you want to ask if you can work in the computer room instead?"

"Why would I want to do that? At least if I'm sitting out I can perv on the girls."

I laughed. "I just thought you could send off the replies from Carrie Edwards."

He looked blank.

"You know – *PINK*? Mum's mag? Chick problems?"

"Oh, right. It's been a mad weekend. My mates from the Bombers caused a riot in the hospital before they got kicked out. Sorry, I totally forgot about this school stuff.

Anyway, I thought we didn't have any answers?"

"We do now. I worked on them over the weekend ... on my own." He seemed totally unimpressed. "We'll tell the first one to stay put and the second to get help from school."

He shrugged. "What does Casey say?"

"I don't give a stuff."

He looked surprised but he didn't say anything.

"Do you think Casey is acting weird lately?" I asked.

"Yeah, I guess. His phone is always off and he was a no-show at the hospital. I haven't even told him about making the Bombers yet."

"Maybe he thought you had enough friends there," I said pointedly, unable to resist taking a shot. It went over Ed's head.

"You can never have enough friends, Tommo. How about those Bomber guys? They're full-on nutters, aren't they?" He didn't seem to notice I was avoiding an answer.

"Here are the replies to the problems," I told him.

"OK, I'll go type them up and send them to your mum."

I handed him the A4 sheet. "And remember to use the spellchecker."

He grinned and limped off.

Later, I saw Amy for the first time since our Darcy letter lesson. We were almost keeping pace with each other, not speaking and hurrying to class. Noticing my shoelace was untied, I dropped to fix it and she moved several steps ahead. I watched her walk away from me and, just as I was about to rise, she turned round to check out where I was. It wasn't half obvious. Her face went pink when she realized that I'd caught her.

Encouraged by her embarrassment, I sprinted to catch up.

"Hey, Jonesy. What's going on with you?" I wanted to put my arm around her shoulders but I didn't dare.

"Get lost, Tommo."

"Oh, come on, Amy, don't be like that to a guy who writes the best letters in the class."

"I don't think so," she said.

"I know so. I—"

"You know what, Tommo?"

I spun around to see Casey right behind me. Amy took advantage of my surprise, flashed him a bright smile and scurried off.

"Did I just hear you tell Amy that you wrote that letter?"

"I might have hinted at it."

He looked bemused. "If it was you, I'm not paying. Someone helped you with it."

"I was just mucking around with her."

He laughed. "You've got no chance there, mate."

"Do you want to bet on that?"

"Nah, I can't keep taking your money." He fell into step with me and I was ridiculously pleased to have the old Casey beside me, not that he stayed for long.

"Did you hear Ed's news?"

"Yeah. I called him on the weekend," he said hurriedly and changed the subject. "Did we answer those questions for the magazine?"

I told him what I'd arranged with Ed, half-expecting him to protest because he hadn't seen the answers for himself, but he didn't. I left him at the door of my History class and he said he'd catch me later.

"Can't make Ziggy's today, though."

He was off before I could ask him why but I wasn't interested in his reason. What I really wanted to know was why he'd lied about contacting Ed.

Neither of them was at school on Tuesday. I was still annoyed with Casey, so I didn't even bother trying to call him. No doubt he'd show up when it suited him, acting like nothing had happened again. I did try Ed's mobile around nine-ish. When it rang out, I had a go on his landline. He finally picked it up after about ten rings and I could hear voices in the background and loud music.

"Ed," I shouted.

He hesitated. "Ed who? I don't know anyone called Ed except myself."

"Is that supposed to be funny?"

"Are you? Come to think of it, who are you anyway?" His voice was slurred. In the distance I heard someone calling his name.

"It's Tommo."

"Tommo! Tommy, mate! Why did you just call yourself Ed?"

"I didn't."

"Come on over. We're just having a couple of beers."

"Where's your mum?"

"Gone. Gone up the coast yesterday afternoon to Gran's.

Come on. Get over here and have a drink with me and the boys."

"Nah, Ed. I was just checking to see if you were OK."

"I am, mate, I am – it's all good. Was going to come in today but a few of the guys came round last night and crashed. I was still a bit wasted this morning."

"You're still a bit wasted tonight, Ed."

He laughed. "I'm just telling the guys about Rhona's party on Saturday. Marty says he'll get our grog but it'll cost us an extra sixpack."

"You already told us that."

He giggled "Well, here's something I haven't already told us – Casey's brother's a fag." He hiccupped. "Zupposed to be a secret."

I froze. He continued to giggle then he paused to puff on something.

"I've been keeping that to myself for ages." He snorted with laughter. "If you ever tell Casey, you know I'll kick your head in."

I tried to play it casual. I needed to find out how much he knew.

"Know what, Ed?"

He took another long draw and probably blew smoke down the phone. I felt the urge to cough. "That's right. Not a word, Tommo."

How did Ed know about Mikey? Before I could ask any more questions, he said, "Well, got to go, mate. I'll see ya at school tomorrow and remember, shhhhhhhhhhhh." He belched a huge laugh and hung up.

I tried Casey. His phone was switched off. I was about to admit defeat and go to bed when my own mobile beeped.

It was a text from Lena.

Are you awake? Can you talk?

I responded immediately.

Yes.

My phone rang shortly after.

"Hey, Leens, what's up?

"Hi, Tommo. I'm really sorry to bother you about this but it's Casey again. I haven't spoken to him in days and he just isn't answering his phone. Do you know anything? Is there something going on?"

I decided to be partially honest. "I guess so. He's been acting weird with everybody but I don't really know why."

"Is it me? Does he want to break up with me?"

"I don't know, Lena."

"Does Ed know anything?"

Ed knew something all right.

"Look, Ed may have noticed something's off, but he's got his Bombers thing happening at the moment, so I doubt he'll be any help." Don't know why I was covering Ed's back. Habit, I guess.

"I just want to know where I stand, Tommo." Her voice sounded small.

"I know, Leens."

"Can you ask him tomorrow? Can you get him to call me?"

"Sure."

"Thanks, Tommo. I'm glad I called."

"Me too."

"How's Britney? Did she work it all out?"

"Oh, yeah, she's happy."

"Good. Glad I could help you for once. Anyway, I'll see you tomorrow. Bye."

I wanted to keep her on the line.

"Yeah, she was happy, but she's got another problem now."

"What?" Her voice was low and husky. I stretched out on my bed.

"She ... er ... her period's stopped." It was the best I could come up with at short notice.

Lena gasped. "Oh, no, does she think she's pregnant?"

I sat back up. I couldn't have a pregnant cousin. That would be way too complicated. I wondered if there were other reasons for stopped periods. It was time to find out.

"No. Definitely not pregnant."

"Well, there are lots of other reasons for missing a period."

"Yeah, that's what I told her, like..."

"Stress and poor diet," she interrupted.

"She certainly has been stressed about her brother."

"Tell her to go see her doctor."

"Yeah, I will." I was busily thinking if I could get away with another dilemma for Brit – a zitty face, a crush on a teacher – when she said, "Good luck with it. I have to go."

"OK, bye." I knew I'd have to nip this addiction to Leens in the bud before it got messy.

Downstairs a door slammed shut. "Tommy?"

"In my room."

Mum appeared at my door a few seconds later. "Everything OK?"

I nodded. Her cheeks had a wine flush. It was a good sign. If she'd had time to share a drink with someone, her life must be a bit better.

"What did you have for dinner?"

"I made an omelette."

She raised a pencilled eyebrow. "Well, I'm glad to see you're pulling your finger out to look after yourself at last. Dad taught you to cook for a reason, and you take after him. You're a great cook."

"Yes, but I prefer it when someone else does the hard work."

"Like me, you mean?"

"No, definitely not like you. Like the takeaway shop until Dad gets back."

"Good job your father can't hear you."

"How's the deadline going?"

"We're almost there, after a lot of problems."

"So it's all good now?"

She smiled and dropped down beside me on the bed. She put her arms around me and her cheek was soft against mine.

"Yes, it's all good."

I closed my eyes and inhaled the familiar smell of her perfume. I felt like I was five again. I love how she can always make me feel that way.

20

Mrs Lennon was away on Wednesday and to our horror, the Bagpipe Bitch was filling in. She barked out instructions for the work that Mrs Lennon had left and the entire class fell immediately quiet.

"Hey, Casey?" I whispered.

He scribbled furiously and ignored me. I gave up.

Halfway through the lesson, I noticed him checking his phone. It was on silent as usual but someone had evidently sent him a text.

"Was that Ed?" I whispered.

He waved me away impatiently as he thumbed his reply. A few seconds later, it happened again.

I checked to see what Mrs McKenzie was doing. Her eyes were on her desk. I snuck another glance at Casey, seeing a little smile form around his mouth when he squinted at the screen.

"What's he saying then? You know he wasn't at school either yesterday, don't you? And when I called him last night, he sounded out of it." I thought about adding that Ed also seemed to know about Mikey but gut instinct told me this wasn't a good time.

Casey's fingers stopped moving for a second. "It's not Ed," he told me and finished his message.

"Is it Lena? She's been looking for you." I didn't want it to be from her.

He pulled the kind of face I make when I run into the spider's web and I couldn't tell if his distaste was for Lena or me. Either way it was infuriating. Who died and made him so important all of a sudden? I knew I should back off. He didn't want to tell me who he was texting and all this fishing was making me look a bit desperate. I decided to act like I didn't care, but my mouth had another idea. "Well, who is it, then?" I blurted it out.

"Sh." He checked to see where the teacher was before adding, "It's a mate, OK?" His look was a cold warning to drop it.

But we're your mates, Ed and me.

I was saved from actually voicing this pathetic thought when his phone buzzed another message through. He smiled when he read it and answered.

"Kieran Donnelly, did your phone just go off?" Mrs McKenzie was on her feet.

Kieran bobbed in his seat as she moved towards him, her hand outstretched. Short of making a run for it, which I bet he was considering, there was nothing he could do.

"You know the rules. All phones have to be checked into

the school office first thing in the morning. I'll have to confiscate it now."

"But it was on silent, Miss," he protested.

"Not by my standards," she barked.

I suspected she'd have trouble with those standards in a graveyard at midnight. Beside me, Casey was sneaking his mobile back into his trouser pocket. So were at least half the class.

"Who calls a student in the middle of the school day anyway? What can be so important that it can't wait till 3 p.m.?" McKenzie demanded.

No one was game enough to respond. "I mean, it can't be your parents, Donnelly. Surely you're way past your mammy checking that you've remembered to wear clean underpants?"

A few kids who didn't have the Bagpipe Bitch regularly laughed. The rest of us knew better. Her eyes darted around, halting when they reached Carla, who had been one of the first to giggle. "It wasn't that funny!" she snapped, eyeing Carla up and down.

Carla's giggle died in her mouth. Confusion and embarrassment attacked her face like two frenzied painters. It only took seconds for her to become puce and crumpled. McKenzie eyed her like she was an offensive piece of modern art before turning back to Kieran.

"If I find anyone else on a mobile this lesson, there will be big trouble," she told us and naturally we believed her.

Kieran's head went down for a bit then suddenly he whipped around sending Casey and me a rueful smile. We both gave him that "bad luck, mate" kind of nod and he seemed happy with the empathy. As he turned back to his work though, I began to wonder if Kieran had in fact been texting Casey. He's a good bloke, I suppose, but we don't have much to do with him. Why would Casey be sending secret messages to Kieran?

As I was considering the possibility, another quick movement at the front of the class caught my eye. It was Amy Jones. She was looking straight at us with a very sexy smile. Weird that when she did that, all thoughts of Lena disappeared. I decided to play it cool so I only gave her a little wink. She made a pretence of scowling and shaking her head like I was a try-hard, but I know she totally believed I'd written the Darcy letter. She was into me.

When the bell went, Casey grunted something about needing to be somewhere and was off. I tried to catch up to Amy as we left the room but she was out of there as fast as Casey. I grinned. She was playing hard to get. Girls love to do that.

I looked around for Ed in the yard at recess and was told that he'd missed school again today. I tried calling him but his phone was off. I needed to catch up with him soon. I wanted to know how he'd found out about Mikey.

I knew Casey wouldn't be at Ziggy's after school but Ed had a regular shift on Wednesdays, so I figured I would definitely catch him there.

I didn't. Sue caught me instead.

"Where's your mate, then?" she barked as I got to the counter.

"I don't know," I said truthfully.

"His mobile's been off for two days and he's not answering his landline. He was supposed to help me with two kids' parties last night. Has he gone away somewhere?"

Just as I was floundering for an answer, I remembered Ed's leg. "Did you know he hurt his leg last weekend and was in hospital?"

She looked shocked and immediately softened. "Is he OK? He didn't break it, did he?"

"Nah, but he's going around on crutches," I lied.

"Then why the hell didn't he call?"

"He's on strong painkillers. Maybe he forgot. His mum's away so he's getting by on his own. He's probably just a bit disorganized this week."

"I suppose it's not like Ed to let anyone down, is it? I should have known there must have been a reason."

I agreed, handing over the cash for my cheeseburger. But as I squashed myself into one of the plastic chairs that Ed hates so much, I found myself wondering if what she'd said was still true. The old Ed was reliable but I wasn't so sure about the new Ed, the one who hung out with guys called Crazy and Marty. Did I really know him, or Casey for that matter, any more? If so, why was I sitting here on my own with only a cheeseburger to keep me company?

A wave of self-pity broke over me, leaving a slow rumbling anger in its place. I tried to deal with it by thinking about who I was really mad at and decided it wasn't Ed. So what if he was off spending time with his new footy mates? Dad was right. He had to find his feet at the Bombers. He planned on making a living with them. His path to a life after school was appearing a bit sooner than mine and he needed the space to explore. Maybe Casey had worked this out already and that's why he didn't seem too concerned about Ed and his new best mates. If so, he should have let me know what was going on with Ed. We used to talk about stuff like this all the time.

It was definitely Casey who was pissing me off. He had no reason to be acting like this. So what if Mikey is gay? The Caseys would get over it eventually. It was time I let Casey know he was being a tosser.

The cheeseburger flipped in my stomach, urging me to leave. So I did, with a wave to Sue, and headed for Casey's place. I needed to talk and he would listen. That's how it was going to be.

21

By the time I'd turned into Casey's street, I was fired up. I strode past his neighbours' houses and stopped outside his place. As always, it made me think of blackberries and whipped cream – Mum's favourite dessert – with its bluey-black paintwork and pristine white trim. No bird dares to shit on Casey's house; mildew holds its breath and creeps by to settle on the neighbours' places instead and local possums see it as a kind of ground zero. Many a furry brother has been "returned" to nature by Mr C.

As I marched up the winding drive, I began to feel uneasy. I stopped and squinted at the garden. The green lawns were meticulous, not a weed in sight. The flowerbeds were bursting with colour and blossoms floated in the water feature just the way Mrs C liked them. I frowned. Something wasn't quite right with the picture. And then I spotted it. Sneezy was gone! His rock by the pond was empty. I spun around to check out the big fern. Yep, the butterfly on a stick was missing too. In fact, Mrs Casey's entire collection of garden ornaments had disappeared. Puzzled, I climbed the steps to the front porch and held my breath at the sight of four pairs of mud-caked shoes sprawling on the polished boards. I searched for the porcupine shoe rack that Mrs C insists we use. Had that been nicked too? No, he was still there, looking a bit naked.

Before I could ring the bell, the door was thrown open.

"Oh… it's you, Tommy," Mr Casey confirmed. I was glad he did because I wasn't sure of anything at that moment. His tall thin frame seemed to stoop a little as he stood there with his hand on the door, blocking my way. A gust of air blew the stale smell of bacon and burnt toast through the house. What was going on here?

"Just came to see Casey," I told him, reaching down to take off my shoes.

"You needn't bother." He waved absently in the direction of my feet. This was seriously weird. Did he mean I couldn't see Casey or I didn't have to take my shoes off? Mrs C would kill us both if I didn't. I looked down at his feet. His shoes were on. I wasn't that brave. Neither was he. It struck me again that this wasn't normal.

"Don't bother with your shoes. She's gone."

"Oh, right. To the shops?" I stood up. The minute I spoke I knew I'd put my foot in it. His eyes looked like grey bolts and his lips were tight.

"Sorry, I… Is Casey here?" I tried again.

"No one's bloody here." He stepped closer, breathing beer all over me. "And do you think I bloody well care about that? Do you?" He didn't bloody well care about my answer, thank

God. He didn't wait for one. "If Steve wants to go off with them, he can. I've had enough of the three of them." It took me a second to realize he was talking about Casey. Casey was going away? It was news to me. He peered at me and suddenly poked my chest with a ragged fingernail. "You tell Steve from me. You tell him I don't need any of them." He turned, went back inside and slammed the door.

Things began to make more sense now. Mrs C had done a runner with her garden ornaments. To where though? To Mikey's place? And apparently Mr C couldn't care less. I was shocked. Why hadn't Casey told me?

Memories of his protests about me not really knowing his family came flooding back. I felt resentful again. Of course I didn't understand. Hard to, when no one explains anything.

I made my way back down the driveway. As I turned to shut the gate, I caught a glimpse of the Hills hoist in the back garden. Normally heaving with washing, it looked like a dancer without a tutu, moving self-consciously as the wind toyed with a couple of Casey's shirts. They seemed to tell me much more about the Caseys' new world than all Mr C's angry ramblings.

I took the short cut through Arnold Park, which would bring me out a block away from my place. It was getting dark now and thoughts of Casey were crowding my mind. He needed to explain what was going on. As I reached the pond, a sudden giggle alerted me to the fact that I wasn't alone. I looked around and decided that it had come from the left. There was a bench there, half hidden by a massive bush.

I peered through the foliage and could just make out two figures in the fading light: definitely a chick and probably a guy. Their faces were close together. They looked as if they'd just come up for air. Normally, I would have walked on because I'm not in the habit of spying on couples pashing in the park, but something about the girl made me stop. I moved closer, being careful not to be seen. I was right. I did know the girl. It was Rhona Smith. Judging from the way she was giggling and the way her blouse was rearranged, her party had started early and Casey was the only one who knew.

22

Mum was home when I got back.

"Tommy?"

"Yeah?"

"Can you come in here?"

I dropped my bag outside her study door and entered.

"Tommy, I... Good Lord. What's up with your face?"

"Nothing." I made an effort to stop scowling. I didn't know what to think about the sight I'd just witnessed. What was Casey up to? Rhona is hot, there's no denying it, and really popular at the moment because of her party, but what about Lena? Why was he cheating on Lena? I remembered her cute nose in the cafe. I would never cheat on Lena if she were mine. It was a random thought but it took hold. Why couldn't she be? He was doing the dirty on her. We got on great. I really liked discussing the problems stuff with her, but I fancied Amy more. Amy was unpredictable. I liked that.

"Has something happened?"

"No. I'm just tired, that's all."

"Tired from what?" She spun around in her chair.

"Nothing. I'm fine." I made an effort to lighten up.

She gave me another suspicious look before turning her attention to her red leather-bound diary. "Well, I've just realized I've got pre-launch drinks on Saturday evening."

I squirmed at the mention of the mag. All this Casey stuff had taken the fun out of it. I began to feel worried too. Had she got the answers to the problems? Were they OK or would there be an unpleasant email waiting for Carrie Edwards from Mum tomorrow?

"I know you've got your party then so I need to check where we're both going to be. Did you say something last week about staying at Ed's?"

I nodded.

Was I still staying at Ed's? I didn't know now. Neither Ed nor Casey had mentioned it this week. Mum didn't wait for an answer.

"And none of you will be driving?"

"No."

She nodded her approval. "I suppose it's pointless me asking if Ed's mother will be there?"

"I'm nearly eighteen, Mum," I protested.

She looked at me over the top of her glasses. "Shh! I choose not to think about that, Tommy." She pulled her ponytail into a knot on the top of her head and fixed it there with a silver thing. It made her look younger.

"Don't worry, when you wear your hair like that no one would suspect you've got a seventeen-year-old kid." I flashed her my most dazzling smile. "You don't look much more than seventeen yourself."

"Oh, but I am, and experienced enough to know when I'm being played by you. Now do please answer my question. Will Evelyn Saunders be home on Saturday night?" She stared at me.

Shit!

Then something unusual happened. She broke the stare.

Yes!

It wasn't like her to make such an amateur mistake and naturally I took full advantage as she dropped her gaze back to her diary. I've never been able to look Mum in the eyes and lie but I've got no such problems with the top of her head.

"She'll be out too, but..." I held my breath, hoping that she'd assumed that Mrs S would only be a taxi ride away instead of a plane trip.

I knew I'd got away with it when she exclaimed, "Oh, blast! This meeting with *Vogue* shouldn't still be in here. It was cancelled last week."

"Sorry?"

She flicked the offending appointment with a white-tipped fingernail. How do women get that part of their nails so clean?

"Honestly, nothing gets done properly unless I do it myself."

"But you love Bec. She's the best PA in the business, or at least that's what you say when Dad complains about spending so much money on her Christmas present."

"She'll only be getting a candy cane this year if she keeps stuffing up my diary. Now I'll have to use liquid paper and it messes up my page."

"Don't stress about your page and don't worry about me on Saturday night. Enjoy your drinks. You need a break. I'll keep my mobile on the whole time so you can call me if you want."

She smiled. "As long as you call me when you get back to Ed's place after the party, Tommy. I'll be furious if you don't. And please do be sensible about—"

"Sex, drugs and rock'n'roll?" I quipped.

"Are you having sex?" she demanded, before dissolving into fits of giggles at my horrified protests. "Don't worry, I'm not one bit interested. Your sex life is your father's responsibility. When we flipped the coin for that, I won."

I collapsed into her sofa. "Have you ever lost?"

"Yes, I made the wrong call on 'responsibility for family meals'."

"But you never cook," I protested.

"Exactly. And I'm totally responsible for that."

We both laughed until she noticed my shoes on her sofa. "Feet!"

I hung them over the edge.

"So everything is going OK with the launch?" I fished.

"Yes. I'm sure we'll iron out the last-minute glitches."

"What kind of stuff will be in this magazine?" My stomach felt tight.

"Oh, the usual kind of thing for girls: celeb news, local

interest stories, film reviews, advice."

I seized on that. "What kind of advice? I hope *you're* not giving anyone health advice, Mum. That would be scary. And you could be sued later." I looked pointedly at her ashtray.

"Don't nag me. I'll give them up again next week before your father gets back."

"He'll know."

"Not if you keep your mouth closed! I didn't work on *Castle & Shed* magazine for eight years without learning how to thoroughly detail a room. Trust me, the entire house will be smelling of roses next week. But to answer your question, no, I don't personally advise anybody – we pay people to answer questions and print their responses in the appropriate column."

"Who do you pay?"

"We've got a doctor for the health issues and a psychologist for the social concerns."

I shifted uncomfortably. "But I bet you make up the questions."

"We most certainly do not." She looked surprised. "Why would you think that?"

I ignored her. "Well, do you ever make up the answers then? I mean, what if you don't like what your experts say?"

She shook her head again. "That wouldn't be ethical, Tommy. Our readers trust us and we're obliged to do things properly. Anyway, that's why we pay experts in the first place. I trust them to do their job and it's all above board. We have to be really careful when we print advice and we have to accredit it, you know. It's a legal minefield out there at times." She kicked off her heels and stole a quick glance at her computer screen before saying, "Why the sudden interest in advice columns? Are you sure there's nothing wrong with you?"

I sprang up from the sofa. My head was beginning to throb.

"Come to think of it, I do have a bit of a headache."

She looked alarmed. "I hope you're not coming down with something. I really can't afford to catch a bug this week. Off you go to bed. Take two Panadol and sweat it out. I'll check in on you later."

I lay in bed and fingered my mobile phone. The need to hear Lena's whispering voice was overwhelming. I'd even thought up another Britney problem: poor kid, her life was just a mess at the moment. I got as far as dialling her number and cut off. I just wasn't sure what I wanted. Amy was gorgeous and I definitely had the hots for her, but there's something about Leens. Would it be wrong for me to chase her now I knew about Casey and Rhona?

Then I thought of Amy's sexy smile again and her total disdain for me. Somehow that was even hotter than Leens's voice. I chucked the phone on the chair next to my bed and resolved to leave it there. It took me ages to fall asleep.

23

At school the next morning I made a beeline for Ed who was standing with a crowd around him. Someone was holding the local paper. Ed caught my eye and grinned, waving his own copy of *The Shout* in my face.

"The Edster is famous, mate."

I snatched the paper and began to read.

LOCAL STAR ON THE RISE

The Bombers' talent development scout, Bill O'Grady, has just announced that this year's round of working with local junior clubs has netted two new stars and one of them is seventeen-year-old, Edward Saunders.

Saunders' signing wasn't without incident as it came at the end of a game in which he sustained a leg injury and concussion.

"I didn't need any painkillers after Bill told me the news," Saunders told *The Shout*, claiming to be "stoked".

O'Grady said yesterday, "The Bombers' Youth Development Program is one of the finest in the country. If these lads have the skill and the commitment to play elite sport, we'll be there for them, securing their financial future as well as their sporting one. Ed is one of the most gifted young players we've come across in years."

Saunders will join the club's successful Under Eighteen side. With plans by the NRL to combine teams and have one National Under Twenties league next year, the future looks very bright for our local hero.

"Bet you did need painkillers, superhero," Kieran Donnelly teased.

"Mate, anyone who knows you needs painkillers."

I had to laugh. When his groupies thinned and it was only us, I asked him where he'd been.

He looked a bit guilty. "Here and there."

"You missed your shifts at Ziggy's."

"How do you know?"

"I was stupid enough to go in there. Sue grabbed me."

"What did you tell her?"

"Don't worry, I covered your arse but you better show up there today and look like you've been out of it." I paused. "Oh, sorry, I'm forgetting, you actually have been out of it."

"Yeah, well my leg's been bothering me."

"Cut the bull, Ed. When I last spoke to you, you were off your face."

He stopped and stared at me. "Tommo, if I want a mum, I'll call my own."

I was about to argue my point when he said, "Anyway, I'm back, aren't I? And isn't today our problem page day? I'll log on at lunch and we'll look at the next two chick complaints."

I flinched.

"What? Don't tell me you're not into it any more? We did a great job last week."

"I know."

"So what's wrong?"

I told him what Mum had said about ethics.

"But it's not like we're giving bad advice, is it?"

I had to laugh at the "we". The plan to give us something we could do together had died in the arse. I was the one with all the answers and, to be really honest, after what Mum said last night, I didn't really care about proving a point any more. The only thing I was getting out of it was spending time with my mate's girlfriend. Was I ready to give that up?

I looked at Ed. "No, I guess not. Don't worry. I'm sure it's all OK." But it wasn't really. Mum being held accountable for our advice was a big enough nightmare but what if we were actually giving bad advice and someone took it? My head pounded as Ed said his goodbyes.

I headed for the stairs to the second floor and, as I looked up, I saw Casey standing there. I thought immediately about my visit to his house. His shirt was definitely creased. All the anger I still harboured evaporated. I should give him a chance to explain what was going on. Perhaps I should tell him I'd witnessed his little session with Rhona and he could explain that too. But I couldn't get the right words out when I tried. Eventually, the voice in my head yelled: "It's only Casey, for God's sake, just be yourself!" I took the stairs two at a time, words swarming in my head like bees. Sure, they might have a sting in them when I finally confronted him – I was entitled to that – but in the end it would be sweet.

Before I could speak, he said, "Dad said you came round."

"Yeah."

There was a long pause. "What's up?" He smiled weakly.

Now was my chance. He looked like he wanted to talk. "I was just—"

"Hi, Tommo. Hi, Casey." I looked behind to see Lena and Amy climbing the stairs. Lena joined me on the step below Casey and, in an amazingly deft movement, she sidestepped me and ended up in front, facing him.

"Hi, Leens," I squeaked, toppling back a step, but I may as well have been invisible. Her eyes pinned Casey to the wall. I've never seen him look so uncomfortable. Behind me Amy tutted at my apparent clumsiness.

"Is there something wrong with your phone?" Lena grilled him.

Her voice sounded tight and I was betting she had that scary smile on her face that lots of women get when they're pretending to be reasonable but they're really baying for your blood. I could only see her back. Her bra strap was outlined through her white shirt. I focused on it while Casey stalled.

"Er ... I don't think so. I just haven't charged it for a while, I guess."

She stared at him through a pause. "You guess?" Her shoulders stiffened. I knew her boobs would be sticking out now so I strained my neck to look at them. "Well, here's what I *guess*, Casey..." I knew this was going to be bad.

As she took a deep breath, I glanced behind and tried to judge how fast I could cover the stairs down, but Amy was blocking my escape route. I gave her a nervous smile, raising my eyebrows in a "let's get out of here" gesture, hoping for solidarity. Surely she didn't want to witness an embarrassing domestic either?

But apparently she did. She ignored me completely. I could have pushed past her but that would have meant touching her and that just wasn't an option. I wasn't ready to go for that kind of intimacy yet – not on the school stairwell – but I was acutely aware that we were close. I tried not to openly snort her perfume, which really did smell awesome, but I supposed from the sneer on her face, I must have started to breathe heavily.

Lena's rising voice made me turn back to Casey.

"… that's what I guess, Steve Casey." Damn! I'd totally missed what she'd guessed.

"It's not true, Leens. I'm fine. We're fine. I promise." Casey's voice was soft and low. Amy gasped. No doubt she thought Casey was spinning Lena a line. Trust her not to give the guy the benefit of the doubt. She'd probably schooled Leens in all her feminist crap and was disappointed that Casey was cutting through it with his sweet-talk.

Casey ruffled Lena's hair. His fingers released a wave of floral scent as they played with her curls. Like Amy, she smelled great too. For a crazy minute, my hand almost shot out to join his. I turned back to Amy. Her lips were slightly open and I could just see the tip of her tongue resting on a crooked front tooth.

"I didn't know your front tooth was crooked," I blurted out and immediately regretted it. It was the pressure of being sandwiched between them. I couldn't take it.

"I didn't know your breath smelled," she replied.

What?

I'd had enough. I got over my touching phobia and pushed her out of my way. "Excuse me."

She stumbled a little and moved into the railing to let me by. I had taken two steps down when I realized that she hadn't complained about me touching her. Was that another sign that she really liked me? I was pretty certain she didn't mean to be a bitch to me. I glanced up quickly, trying to catch her in the act of watching me, but she wasn't. She was still waiting patiently on the stairs behind Lena, as Casey told his girlfriend he'd explain everything after school.

I thought about Rhona.

Good luck with that, Leens.

24

I met Ed at lunch in the computer room.

"Over here," he said as he booted up a computer. "Right, let's see what *PINK* has got for us today."

I sat down reluctantly. "Ed, I've changed my mind about this *PINK* thing."

"But I thought we talked about that already?"

"Yes, but…"

"Is it because Casey's chickened out?" he demanded.

"Has he?" This was news to me.

"I guess he has. Let's face it, he wasn't much help last time and he's not here now, is he? Don't sweat it though, he's just a bit off at the moment."

I jumped at the opportunity to talk about Casey. "Yeah? What do you know?"

"Nothing much, mate. He's just got stuff going on, I guess."

"Yeah." I nodded. How did he know about Mikey? I was racking my brains for a way to ask him when a slapping noise caught my attention and I looked up to see Ed thumping his head with the heel of his hand.

"You've forgotten your password again, haven't you?" I sighed.

"You don't know it, do you?"

I shook my head wishing I'd taken Casey's advice before.

"Wait here, I'll go ask a few people from my computer class. They'll remember it." He flashed me a huge Edster grin.

I laughed as he headed off and found myself thinking about Casey again. With two girlfriends going at the same time, there would soon be no one left worth dating. I didn't get what he was playing at. What was he trying to prove? Was he taking out a sort of "chick insurance" against ending up like his brother?

"Got it," Ed said, returning. "The Edster 1." He began typing as I reluctantly shelved my thoughts.

"How could you forget that?"

"I dunno." He looked baffled. "Oh well, at least the first person I asked knew it." He smiled proudly as he logged onto his account and clicked on the latest problems from *PINK*.

To: edwards@mailwatch.com
From: charliesweeney@panpublications.com
Subject: Edition 2. Column

Hi Carrie,

Thanks for your answers last week. They'll appear in next week's first edition.

Here are two more for the second edition.

Don't forget to send me some banking details.

Keep your fingers crossed for the launch next week.

Cheers,

Charlie

Ed beamed. "See, we did a good job. Let's open the attachment."

We did.

Dear Carrie,

I'm 16 years of age and I've just found out that my parents are divorcing. They won't tell me why. I want to cry all the time. People keep telling me I'm lucky it didn't happen when I was a little kid but I still feel like a little kid. What should I do?

Mel (NT)

I read it and thought about Casey immediately. This one was going to be harder to run by Leens. In fact, this one really needed proper advice.

"I think—" Ed began, but I cut in.

"Ed, we have to stop. We know nothing about this stuff. We can't do this."

"Well, you can't maybe, but I sure as hell can. I'm the one around here with the single mum."

I was surprised. I was so used to Ed's silence on the matter of his parents' break-up that I'd forgotten he had the right to an opinion. I waited to hear it.

"I think her friends are right. She is lucky. It's much worse for a little kid to find out his parents are packing it all in. When my dad left us he wrecked everything!" We were both aware that his voice was slowly rising. Questions piled on top of each other in my head, building a ladder that I definitely wanted to climb. At the top I knew I would find out what really made Ed tick.

"Anyway, there's no point in going on about it," he announced with such bleak finality that I lost my footing and tumbled to the ground. In the end all I could manage was one question.

"Where is your dad?"

"Dunno. Neither does Mum, but she keeps a lookout. She doesn't want him back."

"Why did he leave?" I wanted to know and, for the briefest moment, I thought he was going to tell me, but the light in his eyes suddenly clicked off as if they'd been on a timer. And in a heartbeat my chance was lost.

"She booted him out. Doesn't matter why. Anyway, I'm just saying that I can answer Mel's question."

I pretended to scan the screen again, all the time knowing that Ed couldn't answer Mel's question. Someone who refuses to discuss his own life with his best mate shouldn't be doling out wisdom to someone else. It was wrong. And it was wrong for me too. After all these years, I couldn't get Ed to open up to me when it really mattered so I had no right to offer anyone else advice. It was time to abort.

"Look, Ed. I agree you're the most qualified to answer this

problem but I'm pulling the pin on the whole thing now. It's just not right."

If I was expecting a fight, I was disappointed.

"Fair enough. It didn't really end up being the laugh you promised."

I was immediately defensive. "Well, it might have been if Casey had been more into it."

He shrugged. I took my chance to mention Mikey.

"But I suppose he's got a lot on his mind at the moment with Mikey."

His head shot up. "What do you mean?"

"Nothing. I'm just saying Mikey's a touchy subject for Casey at the moment, isn't he?"

He looked around, checking there was no one else in earshot. "How did you find out about Mikey?"

I considered my answer carefully. I could have told him about Casey's late-night phone call but for some reason I wanted to make him sweat. "You told me, mate."

He blinked rapidly like he couldn't process it. "I did not," he hissed.

"You did, on the phone on Tuesday night. You were off your face and you blurted it out."

He was shaking his head. "I didn't."

"How else would I know?" I challenged.

He looked ill. "I can't believe I did that, I just can't believe it."

"That's what a bender with the Bombers will do to you, Ed."

But he was too stunned by his betrayal to argue. "So what did I say exactly?"

"Well, you were laughing and whispering about a secret, then you told me Mikey was gay and if I mentioned it to Casey, you'd kill me."

He didn't reply.

"So you're lucky I didn't. Casey would be pissed if he knew you'd spilled his secret."

He looked confused. "What secret?

"What he told you about Mikey," I prompted.

He shook his head so vehemently, I was sure it would roll off his neck.

"No, Casey doesn't know!" he exclaimed.

Now I was confused. "Well, how did you find out?"

He took a huge breath and released the air slowly as he shifted uncomfortably in his seat.

"I saw Mikey a few weeks ago in town. He was coming out of a pub holding some guy's hand. The guys I was with told me it was a gay bar. They gave them both a bit of a wind-up, actually. It was…" He stopped, deciding not to remember that part.

"Did he see you?"

"Yeah, but I didn't recognize him at first. They were kissing by the time we got close. I called him a sick perv and whistled at him like the rest of the guys. When he turned round, I couldn't believe it was Mikey Casey."

"What did you say?"

"Nothing. I was seriously shocked." He paused. "But not

because he's gay. I mean, I was amazed that I didn't know that about him before then, but I was more shocked that the random stranger I'd been winding up turned out to be my best mate's brother. I dunno, Tommo, it just felt kind of weird, do you know what mean?"

I nodded. "Did you apologize?"

He looked away.

"Guess that's a no, then?"

"I couldn't, Tommo. The guys would have turned on me."

"Your new Bombers mates?" I spat the words out.

He didn't seem to notice my tone.

"So what happened then?"

"Well, he was obviously pissed off, especially when he saw it was me."

"What did he say?"

"He said, 'Does your Mummy know you're out, Ed?' and all the guys started to laugh."

"Then what?"

"I got pissed off. I couldn't let him get the better of me in front of the guys, so I said something about wondering if Casey knew that he had a homo brother."

I kept quiet.

"Then he looked at me as if I was a piece of crap and turned away. I don't think he'll ever speak to me again. He and the other guy headed off and we went on to the next pub. When the guys asked me who he was, I gave them some info about Mikey and Casey but when we reached the club, they didn't seem that bothered any more. I guess they were more interested in getting a round in."

"How come you didn't tell me?" I asked. He looked sheepish and began to stare at the computer again.

"Did this happen the weekend you told us you were at your gran's?"

A slight nod.

"Why didn't you carry out your threat to tell Casey?"

"I didn't threaten anybody," he protested, obviously cut by my choice of words. "I was mad at Mikey for making me look like a tosser in front of my mates and I was stressing about getting asked for ID at the next club: my fake isn't all that good. I suppose I just wanted a comeback that would shut him up. I guess I went too far."

I felt sorry for Mikey Casey. Meeting Ed that night was a massive piece of bad luck. He must have been certain that Ed would tell Casey his secret.

Ed was speaking at me again. "And anyway, I would never have told Casey because he would have flipped. He'd have hated me even if he did eventually find out I was telling the truth. Casey is one of the worst gay bashers in the school."

"He's not any worse than the rest of us, Ed."

"Oh, yeah? When was the last time you broke into Luke Grovner's email account to send a piss-take love letter to a male teacher?"

It took a minute to understand. I stared at him in disbelief. Words wouldn't form.

"Yeah. That was Casey."

"How do you know?"

"I was sitting right next to him in the library at the time."

"Why didn't you tell me?"

He looked down at his hands and played with a ragged nail for a second. When he looked up, there was an indulgent look on his face. "Because you're a safety player, mate."

Was that an insult? Was he saying I was soft?

"I'm so not a safety player," I whispered, barely able to contain my anger.

"You are so. You always do the right thing."

"I'm not the one who cleans up all my rubbish at Ziggy's…" The minute I said it I felt stupid.

He guffawed. "So you walk away and leave your rubbish for Casey to clean up. You're a real bad ass, Tommo."

I was determined to stand my ground.

"Well, what's so outrageous about the stuff you're doing, Ed? Just because you're smoking a bit of pot and getting wasted every weekend? And let's not forget your 'crazy' new mates! They're not so friggin' tough—" I had more to give, but Ed was getting out of his seat. He was sniffing hard.

"This is stupid, Tommo. No one is calling you a pussy, man. I'm just saying that you always seem to draw a line, and Casey and I reckoned the Grovner thing would have been well over it. That's why we didn't tell you," he explained.

"We all draw lines," I protested.

He nodded. "But yours is nowhere near mine, or Casey's."

Seeing I was about to protest again, he shook his head. "Don't worry about it. We're just different, mate." He grabbed his bag and scrambled off.

I turned back to the screen but I had trouble focusing. He hadn't even bothered logging off. I went to do it for him when I remembered the second problem on the attachment. May as well read it. I welcomed the distraction. Whatever it was, it couldn't be a patch on the worries I had now.

Dear Carrie,

My friend and I are thinking about taking a gap year after our HSC but our parents aren't keen. We'd both like to travel and party but we'd also like to do some voluntary work too. Where can we get information on our options?

Ali (Qld)

Bloody hell! What was wrong with the chicks writing to Carrie Edwards? They were all so boring and serious. Where were the ones who wanted advice on the size of their tits, or how to give blow jobs? I clicked out of the screen in disgust.

25

I really did feel bad the next day so I begged off school, which actually isn't like me at all. Mum still seemed more worried about catching my germs before the launch than she was about me.

"Didn't you take something for that headache the other day?" she demanded.

"Yes, but it came back again."

"What is it? Is it just a headache? Do you feel fluish? Take something else, will you, and if you start feeling worse, go to a doctor today." She blew me a kiss and headed out.

I imagined what a doctor might tell me.

Diagnosis: Your friends are toxic.

Remedy: Get new ones.

I didn't want new friends. I wanted the old ones just the way they'd always been, but there was no chance of that now. We were keeping too many secrets. How did we go from being so close, to not really knowing each other at all? Do you get more secretive as you get older? Is it compulsory?

Maybe when you're an adult, there are unwritten rules about what you're allowed to share with certain people and secrets just happen whether you like it or not. Like in *Pride and Prejudice*, when Mr Darcy has all that info about Elizabeth's skanky sister running off with that loser but can't tell her.

Maybe it's a good thing that me and the guys have our own secrets now. Perhaps I should be rearranging the picture I've got of us in my head before piecing it back together again like you do with a jigsaw.

As I sank back into the overstuffed sofa in the living room, a memory floated into my mind. Mum handing me a massive jigsaw puzzle with lots of intricate pieces when I was about seven. There was a picture of an aviary on the lid.

"I don't even like birds," I'd complained to Mum.

"Your grandmother sent it for your birthday, so now you do," Mum snapped.

When I'd eventually stopped sulking about not getting a boogie board and set it up on the table in my room, it had taken ages to complete. I can still remember how good it felt adding that last piece.

"Break it up and rebuild it," Dad said when I'd finished.

But I never did. It was part of my room and I needed it there.

"Do you want a new one?" Mum sometimes asked.

My answer was always the same. "No."

Then one day I came home from school and Mum met me in the hall.

"Darling, I've got some bad news about your jigsaw."

I raced into my bedroom. The jigsaw was in pieces. "An accident, of course. Jan knocked it over when she was dusting," Mum told me.

"Why do we have to have a stupid cleaner, anyway?"

Mum rolled her eyes. "If you need me, I'll be back in my study."

I didn't go to her in tears, even when I felt like it. It was only a dumb jigsaw. I piled it all in its box and it's probably still in the cupboard under the hall staircase.

I never tried it again. I figured it would never look as good as it had that first time.

I hadn't thought about that jigsaw in years but it reminded me of us. Until recently we were a perfect picture, but now we're broken pieces, bundled into a box until someone can be bothered to put us together again.

God, I was depressing myself. It had to stop.

Tomorrow night was Rhona's party and it was going to be awesome. I nodded off to sleep counting all the available chicks in my head that I knew for sure would be there.

When my phone beeped it was late afternoon, judging from the light outside. I yawned and checked the message. A text from Casey.

what time 2morro nite?

This was a good sign. I considered my answer. Eight-thirty? We'd have to get some grog first and nobody wants to turn up at a party too early. You don't want to seem desperate.

I got back to him.

C U outside Pepper Cellars @ 8.30

I waited.

No probs.

If only that were true.

26

I couldn't contact Casey all day Saturday and began to wonder if he would turn up. We had a bye in footy so it's not as though I got to see him at the game.

"How do I look?" Mum asked around eight, spinning in my room on ruby stilettos.

"Tall."

"Too tall? Should I wear the crimson ballet slippers instead?"

"Go with what feels better."

She guffawed. "Now that's funny." She eyed herself again in my mirror and nodded. "I'll stick with the Jimmy Choos."

"The Jimmy whos?"

"Never mind." She was already out the door and halfway down the stairs.

"Your bum looks big in that," I called.

"Just make sure you stay in touch tonight, or your bum will be the one in question. It's never too big for a smack. Have a lovely time. Bye."

The front door slammed. I wasn't far behind her. Checking I had my wallet and phone, I left about ten minutes later and headed for Pepper Cellars. Neither Casey nor Ed was there yet. Not wanting to loiter outside in case anyone noticed me, I decided to take a walk around the block.

There's an art to acquiring grog when you shouldn't. The most obvious way to go is the fake ID. The problem is that nowadays some clubs are using a blue light thingo, which picks up even the smallest cut and paste job. I blame shows like *CSI*. Everyone likes to think they're a forensic expert.

The next option is to grab someone who is old enough to be legit, but not too old that they'll feel responsible and dob you in.

When I got back from my circuit, Casey was waiting across the street. I ambled over to him. He looked at his watch. "What time did Ed say he'd be here?"

My face fell. "He didn't. I haven't spoken to him since Thursday, have you?"

He shook his head. "Isn't that mate of his coming to get us what we need?"

I nodded.

"So where are they, then?"

"Dunno. I never know much about where you and Ed are these days."

"What's that supposed to mean?" He was snapping again as he frantically texted on his phone. I suddenly felt tired. What was the point of antagonizing him? We were supposed to be going to a party. His message was returned and he swore.

"What?"

"That was Ed. He said he'll meet us there. He's doing something first."

"But what about the beer?"

"He told us to get our own."

I sighed. "So we'll just have to pick someone then?"

"Shouldn't be too big a problem. It is Saturday night."

We moved away from the door of the bottle shop to avoid suspicion and crossed the street to wait for an approachable candidate in silence.

"We have to can the Carrie Edwards thing," I said, trying to make conversation.

"Why? Did your mum find out?"

"Nah. I just don't feel good about the legal stuff." I started to tell him about what Mum had told me about ethics. Of course, I completely omitted the fact that I was using it as a way to spend time with his girlfriend. While we were talking a car drew up and parked outside the bottle shop. A white Fiesta with new driver P-plates. Promising. When the doors finally opened, three girls came gaggling out. They were only a couple of years older than us, all blond and barely dressed. I looked at Casey and he winked. "Let's do it."

We sauntered across the street to their car.

"Hi, ladies," Casey said, giving them his best boyish grin. "Do you reckon you could do us a bit of a favour?"

"What?" The spokeswoman was the one who had been driving. She looked great in a tight skirt and boots. She was squashed into a green sleeveless top. It made her boobs look big. Judging from her giggling friends, this was not their first alcohol stop of the evening.

"Just wondering if you could help us with our shopping," Casey told her.

"How old?" She was obviously familiar with the request.

"Eighteen next month," Casey lied, grinning again. She seemed to like him.

"So where are you guys off to tonight?"

"Private party," I said.

"That's a shame." Her friends hooted behind her.

"You need any dates?" one of them asked, taking Casey's arm.

"What about you? You're cute too." The smallest of the girls was standing up close to me. Her hair was piled up on her head. Her top was cut low over shorts. Her high wedges did a little to disguise her height but they weren't miracle workers.

"You're pretty cute yourself," I lied. From the corner of my eye I could see Casey flirting with the girl who had grabbed him. She was facing him now and had both hands on his chest. She stepped into him and nuzzled his ear. He laughed loudly. It was his false laugh. He was working it.

Designated Driver seemed put out. "Come on, you two," she snapped. "Let's get our drinks and get out of here."

"Can you get us what we need?" Casey asked her, shrugging off the blond leech who was sucking the blood out of his ear.

"Oh, I can get you what you need." Her voice was suddenly husky.

Casey flashed her another killer grin. "A case."

"Of what?" she asked, tilting her chin. Man was she hot.

"You choose," Casey said, folding a fifty lengthwise and passing it to her slowly.

She took it and grinned. "Don't go away now."

As soon as they went inside Casey turned to me. "You owe me some cash."

"Yeah, all right," I said passing him some notes from my wallet. "Jeez, maybe if I had tits, I'd get more respect from you, mate."

He laughed and I felt pleased. We waited patiently a little distance away while the girls seemed to take forever in the shop. Eventually they tripped out laden with grog and we retrieved our beer. Casey seemed up for another flirting session but they'd lost interest in us.

"Don't stay out too late, kids," the sober one said, handing over our case. The others screeched with laughter as they got back into the car.

We headed south down Hastings Street in the direction of Rhona's place. As we turned the corner into Rhona's street, I spotted a couple of familiar faces standing on the corner.

"Hey, do you know who those guys are?" I asked Casey.

He shrugged. "Wouldn't have clue."

"They're friends with Ed. They're part of the Bombers crowd. I saw them at the hospital before."

Casey said nothing. He didn't seem too interested.

I nodded as we walked by them. Immediately, one stepped

in front of us blocking the way. My hands tightened on the beer.

He was a fraction taller than me, solid and hard. He would have been a good-looking guy, I guess, if it hadn't been for the acne peppering his face like buckshot. His pupils looked unnaturally large. He was definitely on something.

I grinned at him in a friendly way, trying to play things cool. "You're one of Ed's mates, aren't you? Ed Saunders?"

His eyes narrowed. "What's it to you?"

"I met you at the hospital. Remember? I'm Tommo, his mate from school." The last couple of words stuck in my throat.

He relaxed visibly and stood down. "Right. Thought I knew your face."

"Do you live around here?" I asked politely.

He nodded his head at a house across the street. "Crazy's place," he said. "You off to that Rhona chick's party?"

"Yeah." I didn't want to say too much. I made a move to get going again.

"Who's your mate?" he asked, his attention on Casey now.

"He knows Ed too." I went to introduce him to Casey only to realize that I didn't know his name. "This is Steve Casey," I said instead.

Casey gave him a curt nod. As we made to leave I was aware that he was eyeing Casey closely. We ignored him and began to walk on.

"Hey, Steve, you got a brother?" he called. Casey froze. My

heart sank. I had a feeling that I knew where this was going.

"A fag brother?"

"Keep walking, mate, it's not worth it," I urged.

Behind us the two guys dissolved into fits of laughter.

"Oi, Steve, does it run in the family? Hey, are you and Tommy Boy on a date?"

I pulled at Casey's sleeve and made him move. "Ignore them. Let's just get where we want to go," I muttered.

He moved then like a man in a dream, his feet hardly touching the ground. Their jibes snapped at our heels. When we reached Rhona's driveway and were finally out of earshot, I began to explain.

"Casey, a few weeks ago Mikey was—"

"Shut up! Shut it, you stupid bastard!" He spat the words at me and I froze. Before I could respond, he took the case out of my arms, ripped it open, slung me a sixpack then stormed up to Rhona's front door. It opened in a second, swallowing him up.

I stood under the light from a lamppost at Rhona's gate. Just me and the moths. What a fun party this was going to be.

27

My first instinct was to go after him, tell him to chill and possibly have the honest conversation that we'd both been avoiding for too long.

Instead, I slumped onto a bench on Rhona's front lawn and opened a beer. I gulped it down. The cold liquid barely touched my tongue but it still left a bitter taste. I tossed the empty into the dark and opened another. Behind me the house seemed to throb. Music was bursting through every orifice.

I was getting so sick of it. Casey's moods were seriously pissing me off and Ed's disappearing acts were becoming a joke. I gulped the beer angrily.

"Hey, Tommo, why aren't you inside?" A figure was approaching the house. I made an effort to calm down. It was Kieran Donnelly.

"Just about to wander in," I told him, throwing the second bottle after its mate.

"Where's Ed? Casey?" He was looking around as though expecting them to jump out from behind a bush.

"I told them I'd meet them in there," I lied.

He reached into his rucksack. "Beer?" he offered.

"Might as well," I said, taking it from him. My own bottles were crammed in my pockets. We made the journey to the front door together. It was thrown open before we knocked and two people came tearing out.

"Don't you dare," a girl shrieked and took off down the driveway.

The guy following her with a high-power water gun was laughing.

"Rhona must have a pool," Kieran said, nodding at the water gun.

"Or a younger brother."

"Or both," he added.

This conversation was more excitement than I could stand. Quickly I got my bearings, muttered a "thanks" for the beer and headed into the kitchen. I was feeling a bit light-headed now. The buzz was good but I didn't like the sour taste in my mouth. Time to find a Coke, or something just as sweet.

The room was full of people I didn't recognize, flitting around in the dim light. Every surface was covered with glasses and bottles. There was an unopened litre of Coke on the white island bench but it felt warm. I was trying my luck in the fridge when someone called my name. I looked behind me, beyond the kitchen to a sliding door that led out onto a large deck. Lena was peering in through the flyscreen.

I waved to her, abandoned my search for a soft drink and took another beer from my pocket instead. When I went out onto the crowded deck, she was standing by the rail with Amy.

"Where's Casey?" It was an eye interrogation.

"Dunno." I tried to look away.

"Did he come with you?" The slight thickening of her voice and the five empty flavoured vodka bottles by her feet told me that she and Amy had been here a while.

"Yeah, but he got the shits and headed off on his own." I looked around. "How big is this place anyway? He must be here somewhere." I'd have to find him myself to get the rest of my grog.

"It's pretty big. What did he get the shits about?" Lena asked.

"Who knows? It doesn't take much to set him off these days."

"There's something going on with him, isn't there, Tommo?" She put her hand on my arm. "Tell me what you know." She was wearing a black dress and massive heels that made her a lot taller than usual. Her eyes were level with mine. They were shimmery with make-up and pleading. She looked great.

"I'll see you later," Amy interrupted. I turned to focus on her. She looked even better.

"You sure will," I agreed. She continued to direct her attention to Lena and didn't even bother acknowledging me. Still playing hard to get, obviously. She was in tight jeans and an orange top that tied around her neck. It wasn't much bigger than a handkerchief. I wanted to say something funny about blowing my nose on it, but I didn't quite get it together in time before she disappeared into the crowd.

Lena was pouring herself another drink. "Please tell me what's going on."

"I'm not sure." I was stalling for time. Should I tell her about Mikey? Or should I just tell her I might fancy her if I got nowhere with Amy? My eyes felt heavy. Dance music pounded inside my head. I swallowed some more beer. Screams of laughter came from the garden below and the distant sound of splashing confirmed that there was indeed a pool down there somewhere.

I turned away from Lena and peered into the darkness. A tree-lined path, lit only by solar-powered lights positioned along the ground, led away from the main house. Beyond it, a corner of the garden was illuminated. Must be where the pool was. I turned back to Leens. "Jeez, it's huge, isn't it?"

She didn't reply. I stopped slugging the beer and leaned against the glass deck fence. All the while Lena eyed me, waiting patiently on my reply.

A warm breeze drifted through and a chime tinkled just above my head. I looked up at the string of silver stars dancing in the wind and suddenly I couldn't hear anything else except their jingling music. I watched, mesmerized as the tiny pieces of metal glimmered when they caught the light from the kitchen. The sound made me feel sad.

"Tommo."

But I didn't need any more prompting. "It's all turned bad, Leens."

Her eyes went wide.

"The guys and me … the whole thing … it's over." A lump was forming in my throat. I washed it down with a long slug from my beer bottle and burped. "Ed's got new friends and Casey's got family troubles and can't cope." She began to interrupt me but I went on. "Poor Casey. He flips out at the first little bit of grief that comes his family's way so we've all got to feel sorry for him. He's pathetic." I was pointing at her. "And we don't have much time left, Leens … we just don't. We'll all be moving on soon … you know? 'Swhat my dad says and he's always right." I hiccupped.

"What kind of family problems?"

I ignored her and shifted my position against the fence. I found myself sitting on my bum, not quite sure how I got there. Maybe I'd been pushed.

I glanced around suspiciously before going on. "Just think about me. What am I going to do when they're gone? And how ungrateful are they, after everything I've done for them, eh?" I squinted up at her. She crouched down beside me.

"What kind of family problems has Casey got?" she asked.

"Big! Enormous! Massive ones. Secrets." Her face swam out of focus and her eyes looked like big bug eyes. I started to giggle.

"Look, stay here for a bit, Tommo. I'm going to find Casey and we'll come back and get you."

"Tell him to bring back the grog he stole from me." I waved

her off. I tried sucking on my beer again but nothing came out. Some bastard must have finished it off. I squinted up at all the giants. They looked guilty. Never mind. I'd go and get another one in a minute after I'd rested my eyes. That sounded like a good plan.

28

"I can't believe you're sleeping!" A voice barked in my ear. I opened my eyes just about the same time as someone kicked my feet.

"Ahhh!" My head jerked back, my hands shot out and I made a half-hearted effort to leap to my feet. I failed and slumped back down.

"Tommo, how long have you been here?" A sweet perfume engulfed me.

"Mum?"

"As if." Another thump to my foot. It caught my ankle and the sharp pain brought me to my senses. Suddenly, I was wide awake and looking up into the scowling face of Amy Jones.

I bounced up successfully this time and instantly regretted it. My mouth felt dry and my head throbbed. I struggled to get my bearings. It was dark and party music was blaring. Slowly, I began to take in snippets of conversation around me:

"No way! The best try ever scored by the Bombers was…"

"Hey, Anna, how hot is he? Seriously, I reckon you should…"

"Mate, grab me another beer from the esky…"

"Tommo, where's Casey?"

It took me a few seconds to work out that the last question had come from Amy. I made a conscious effort to focus on her face.

Man, those lips are unreal.

How long had I been out of it? "Probably with Lena," I told her.

"How much have you had to drink?" she asked.

"Not much." I tried to count back. "Maybe four." I didn't bother to tell her I'd swallowed them all in the first forty minutes.

As she glared at me, I held my hand out to her. "Give us a hand up and I'll help you look for them."

She gave me her hand and I grabbed it. It was soft and surprisingly strong.

"I think you need some coffee first."

She was probably right. "Only if you make it."

"Come on, then," she beckoned me to follow. I had no problems with that.

The crowd in the kitchen had thinned out. "What time is it?" I asked.

"Nearly eleven-thirty."

I calculated I'd been sleeping on the deck for almost an hour. I watched her find her way around the unfamiliar kitchen, seeking coffee and cups as I sat plonked on a kitchen stool.

The orange top was backless but it was snug. There were no glimpses of side-on boobs no matter how hard I willed it. We didn't talk as she poured two cups of watery liquid. I gulped mine down, content to just listen to her bangles jangle while she sipped.

Eventually, she said, "Do you know I haven't even seen Rhona yet tonight?"

"Neither have I." What was her point?

"I still have her present in my bag."

Bugger. Casey and I hadn't got her anything. Maybe Ed did and we could add our names to it. I wondered if he'd arrived yet.

"She's the birthday girl. She's probably still doing the rounds," I said and almost at once I had a sudden recollection of the birthday girl doing the rounds with Casey in the park. I wondered if Lena had tracked him down.

Amy smiled at me. It was a smile without an ambush. I sobered up right there and realised I no longer cared about Lena. I gazed at Amy and fell in love.

"Busy party," I said, wondering how to shift from the small talk to the important stuff.

"She knows a lot of people."

"Yeah, she's a cool chick."

Her bangles tinkled again.

"You are too." Best to get straight to it, I guess.

She frowned at me.

"No, seriously," I protested.

"Look, Tommo—"

I held up my hand. "I know … you think I'm full of bullshit and we haven't exactly got on before now but I've always admired you, Amy." The beer buzz was making me fearless.

"Really, Tommo?"

"Yes … really. You're smart and gorgeous and even if you are a bit of a bitch, it's nothing that I can't handle." I reached across for her hand and stroked her wrist. I read in one of Mum's magazines that chicks love that. It seemed to work. Her eyes narrowed with pleasure as she leaned in towards me and looked me straight in the eye as her fingertips firmly pressed my caressing digits to a halt. I gave her a high beam smile of encouragement. This wasn't going to be easy for her but it was time for the Ice Queen to melt. *Drip. Drip. Drip.*

"It was you, wasn't it?" Our faces were close together across the island bench. I didn't have a clue what she was getting at, but her face was flushed and her eyes had gone all dreamy. It had to be good. I wanted to agree with her but decided to hedge my bets.

"I could tell you, but I'd have to kill you," I said in my best James Bond voice.

Her eyes glistened. "You wrote me that amazing Darcy letter, didn't you? It really was you." I noticed that her nipples were pointing at me underneath the handkerchief top.

"Yes, it was me. What can I say? I'm quite good at English, you know."

A deep sigh, then she released the pressure on my hands. Just as I was wondering what to do next, she grabbed them both in hers and moved them to frame her gorgeous face.

An adrenaline rush buzzed through me. I don't think I've ever felt more alive in all my life. Dance music was pumping me up until I thought I'd burst.

"You are beautiful," I told her. I know it was a crap line but I just couldn't stop myself.

Amy smiled and squeezed my hands in hers. "And you're the biggest try-hard I've ever met and..."

I waited for the cute punchline in a happy daze.

"You're a liar. You so did not write that Darcy letter." She let go of me abruptly, picked her cup up and then thumped it down again on the shiny surface. OK, she had a point but I was suddenly in damage control and that's hard when you've got a belly full of beer-flavoured coffee. As I was concentrating on disguising a burp, she pointed a slender finger at me. "Do you want to know something, Tommo?" Her voice sizzled with anger.

I found myself nodding like one of those little gimmicky car dogs.

"Casey wrote that letter."

Never has a head stopped bobbing so quickly. She had to be wrong. Casey didn't even do the assignment. He should have had a detention but Mrs Lennon forgot about him. Casey was with me when I wrote my letter. He helped me. He couldn't have written to Amy too. He knew how I felt about her. He had Lena, why would he want to impress Amy? Then I remembered how his mouth had been making quite an impression on Rhona the other day and felt ill. The room swam around me and I gulped more coffee.

"How do you know?"

She laughed. "He told me right after the lesson. I have to admit, I was shocked, but what can I say? It was beautiful. He's a really interesting guy." She seemed to take pity on me then. "Look, Casey and I have started seeing each other. I know it's going to be hard on Lena, especially as we're friends, but these things happen. Friendships change. Casey and I have found something special: something worth risking friendships for. He's promised to tell her soon and I'm hoping he'll do it tonight, OK?" She flicked her hair out of her eyes and I marvelled at how a gesture that had once turned me wild could annoy me so intensely. There was something cruel about the action that heralded the end of Lena's world.

She'd let my hand drop some time ago and I had the sudden urge to wash it. She really was a piece of work.

"Lena really likes you, Tommo, and anyone can see you're definitely into her." She made me feel like a sleaze.

"Maybe you two can hook up when she feels better. You'd make a great couple." She stood up and smoothed her top down over her jeans.

I wasn't going to let her go without a challenge. "Don't you feel like a bit of a bitch doing this?"

"Don't you feel like a bit of a bastard pretending to have a 'cousin' called Britney?" That took me by surprise. Before I could respond, she said, "When Lena told me about her I asked Casey about your 'cousin'. He reckons he's never heard of her." She glared at me. "It didn't even cross his mind that you were feeding Leens some bullshit story so you could hang out more. That's what you were doing, weren't you? With your best mate's girlfriend?"

I looked away. It was more complicated than that but I'd no chance of explaining myself now. And it could be worse, I guess. Casey could have blabbed about the whole Carrie Edwards scam.

She went on, "And Casey still trusts you because that's the kind of honest guy he is."

Her last comment really got me. Casey honest? Not lately.

"Yeah, right. Anyway, it's not the same thing. I'm not going to hurt her like you and Casey."

It was her turn to look guilty but it didn't last long. "Sometimes you have to make difficult choices in life. It's what happens when you grow up."

"What happens to loyalty to your friends, Amy? Isn't that important when you grow up?"

"Casey is my best friend." Her eyes misted over.

I snorted. "You hardly know him. You haven't got a clue what he's really like."

"I don't expect you to understand this but when it comes to soul mates and real relationships, sometimes people just know."

Enough was enough. "I'll tell you what you don't know. Your soul mate's seeing Rhona Smith as well."

She inhaled sharply and her eyes flashed with hatred. "You liar! I don't believe you." Her hands went up to her face. "I don't have a lot of time for you, Tommy Sweeney, but I've never known you to go out of your way to hurt anyone. That was a really pathetic, low thing to say about your friend."

I held her challenging stare and said nothing.

But she didn't seem quite so sure of herself now. Before I could argue, she threw me another scornful glance and stomped off into the crowd. I dropped my head onto the bench. Stainless steel feels so soothing on your forehead. I could have stayed like that forever.

29

As I wandered through Rhona's cavernous house in search of Casey, I felt pretty sober again.

The news about Casey and Amy was a shock. It explained a lot really. She'd been the one on his mobile last week and obviously he'd written his Darcy assignment after all. I should have known something was up when Mrs Lennon didn't give him a detention. It wasn't like her to make a mistake. And no wonder he was always sneaking off. It's amazing he had any time to spend with me and Ed at all with three chicks on the go.

It must be exhausting. And why go after Amy when he knew I was interested? Was it personal? Or was it nothing to do with me? Was it really the "prove you're straight" thing by chasing as many chicks as possible that I'd considered before? It still sounded better than the alternative: he was just a bastard who didn't give a toss about anyone.

Clearly, none of his chicks knew too much about the others at the moment but eventually they'd want an explanation.

Tough luck, they'd have to get in line behind me because I was getting my answers tonight.

In the living room a couple of kids were watching a DVD.

"Tommo, come and watch this, it's a crack-up," Kieran Donnelly called out.

I didn't feel like laughing. "I'll see you in a bit," I told him, backing out of the room.

Some loud thumping echoed down the hallway.

"Get out of there; she's going to throw up!"

I followed the voice to find a group of people queued outside what had to be the toilet. No sign of Casey or Ed. Some guy I didn't recognize had pushed in and was still pounding on the door while a girl slumped at his feet. As I looked down at her, she lurched forward and vomited on the tiles. Girls squealed and guys swore as they scrambled to avoid her. Just then the toilet flushed, the door opened and two entwined bodies appeared in a lip lock in the doorway.

The door pounder grabbed the female half of the couple, pulling her into the hall. "People are waiting here," he yelled. She staggered forward losing her balance, taking her boyfriend with her. They landed on Spew Girl just as she was giving an encore performance. More loud protests from everyone then Boyfriend sprang to his feet and punched Door Pounder on the chin. As a scuffle broke out, people forgot about the free toilet and gathered round to watch. I didn't bother. I didn't even know them. Where the hell were all these strangers coming from? The big attraction of this party had been that Rhona's parents were up the coast. Now I wasn't so sure.

If her old man had been in the basement somewhere, I think I would have felt better. As I headed upstairs to the first floor, the sound of breaking glass told me things were getting ugly. Not my problem.

The top of the stairs opened onto a wide rumpus area. Kids were either dancing or flopping together on the sofas. I scanned the room: a lot of bodies, a heap of alcohol and too much smoke, but no sign of Casey or Ed. A corridor ran off to the right. I followed it to discover the bedrooms. Actually, I discovered one bedroom, got an eyeful of tits when I opened the door, and pulled it shut again just as Tammy Dannova from my Maths class hurled herself at me, shouting abuse.

I decided against looking in any more bedrooms. Instead, I made my way back through the house and out to the garden where the first person I recognized was Ed's friend from the Bombers. The one who'd mouthed off to Casey earlier in the street. What was he doing here?

I tried to sneak past him but he spotted me.

"Tommo, mate. How're you doing?" He swayed and thankfully the wall was there to catch him. His friendliness was weird but much better than having my head kicked in.

"I didn't know you were invited." I tried not to sound like I was accusing him of anything.

"I guess young Eddy comes in handy at times." His eyes darted. He was still smashed.

I looked around. "Where is Ed?"

He shrugged and the effort made him stagger again. "Last time I saw him he was at the pool with Marty and

Crazy." He took a long draw on something – pot, I guess – before offering it to me. I shook my head. He looked offended and began to scowl.

"Got my own stuff downstairs," I bluffed and made a move past him.

"Right." He thumped my back.

By the time I got to the pool, there was no sign of Ed but plenty of people from school were there. It was a relief to see that the party hadn't been totally taken over by gate-crashers. Just as I thought about where to try next, I spotted a little path leading to the back of the property. I wondered again just how big Rhona's garden actually was. I strolled down it and picked up my pace when I heard yelling. It was coming from a studio building like something from one of Mum's home design magazines with sliding doors and candles all around.

When I got closer, the first person I saw was Amy. She seemed to be fighting gravity as she clung tightly to the door like it was providing her fingertips with oxygen. I stood right behind her and peered inside. A smoking, furious Lena towered over Casey and Rhona, who were on one of those Indonesian bed/sofa things, pretty much naked except for a few tiny bits of clothing, a thin blanket and enough sequined cushions to smother an elephant. Only Amy noticed my arrival. She threw me a scowl then we both turned back to the show.

"And not only that slut, Casey, but you've also been hitting on Amy!" said Lena.

I frowned. If Amy had told her, why wasn't she being yelled at too?

Casey spluttered.

"No, don't you dare try to deny it. Amy's told me everything. We know exactly what you've been doing. You're a sleazy bastard." She turned her attention to Rhona who was now looking for her clothes while clutching at the blanket. She withered under Lena's gaze. "And, as for you, you skank. You…" Her words failed her then and a little cry escaped her lips.

My eyes burrowed into Amy's back. Not even a flinch. Jeez, she was good. How had she managed to get Lena onside so quickly when she'd been just as guilty as Rhona? What about all that talk in the kitchen about her and Casey being soul mates? Bet she left that part out when she fessed up to Leens.

"Come on, Lena, let's get out of here. They're not worth it," she counselled.

Lena turned and spotted me standing there. She burst into tears.

"Leens, I had no idea," I lied, reaching out to her. I couldn't stand to see her like this. She swiped out at me but missed. My eyes searched for Casey and found him. Why didn't he do something? He smirked through an alcohol stupor and slumped back down on the bed. Lena stormed past me into the arms of Amy. They stood sculpted together in the doorway for the briefest of seconds before heading back towards the main house.

"Well, that went well," Casey said to Rhona, who was almost dressed now. Pity.

"You think, Casey?" Then she threw me a poisonous look. Maybe she knew I'd turned up without a birthday present.

"What are you doing here?" she said.

"I was just about to ask him that too." Casey grinned. He was obviously finding everything amusing. I could tell he'd been drinking heavily.

Rhona turned to me. "Can you please get out, Tommo? Casey and I have things to talk about."

Join the queue, Rhona! But I could see there was no point in talking to him when he was like this, so I shrugged and left her to it. She got into his ear even before I made it out the door.

"I was cool with Lena because you told me you would dump her, but Amy Jones? Are you kidding me?" Her voice seemed to get more shrill with every word.

Served him right.

I was halfway back to the house when I heard a weird groaning sound coming from the trees. My first instinct was to ignore it. It was probably just another couple in the bushes and I'd had enough of couples tonight, but I stood rooted to the spot until I finally made up my mind to check it out. I veered off the path and crossed an expanse of lawn that dropped away to a stone wall. A couple of dim lights sticking in a flower-bed revealed a figure lying on the grass. I edged closer and my heart sank. It was Ed. He was on his back. I sprinted the last few steps and dropped down beside him, giving him a shake. His eyes opened but they weren't focusing properly.

"Ed, it's me. Are you OK?"

He didn't seem to hear me at first. I repeated myself and made a lame attempt at getting him onto his feet. He was much heavier than I thought and he slumped back down before I could get a proper grip. The jolt seemed to wake him.

"Ed, it's Tommo. What are you doing out here?"

"Tommo?" he slurred but then his eyes shut again. Did he need help? I wasn't quite sure what to do next. Was he drunk? I looked around but couldn't see any beer bottles or anything. Suddenly, he gave a little snore and curled up into the foetal position. I let out a sigh of relief and only then realized I'd been holding my breath. I stood up and resisted the urge to kick him. He was just as bad as Casey. They were both selfish pricks who'd gone off and done their own thing without giving our plans a second thought.

So much for the boys having a wild night. While they'd been partying, I'd been abused by Amy, brushed off by Leens, abandoned by Casey and Ed and befriended by Kieran Donnelly. I couldn't decide which was worst. What a shit night. It was time to go home. I left him to sleep it off and crossed the lawn again in search of the path.

I must have taken a wrong turn somewhere because I soon found myself in the opening of a smaller garden full of rose hedges. At my end there were two big pots with bushes in them marking the entrance. Down the other end there was a wooden bench and another lawn fell into the darkness beyond it. The narrow paths connecting the garden beds were made of something soft and, like most of the spaces in

Rhona's garden, this one was also lit dimly by solar-powered lights.

I saw Leens and Amy at once. They were sitting on the bench. I knew the others too and felt relieved. These guys would definitely help me with Ed. I decided to interrupt.

Big mistake!

30

Amy had a glass in her outstretched hand and she watched it being filled through half-shut eyes. Lena giggled as it overflowed onto the mulch at their feet. They were with Ed's footy mates.

They looked up at the sound of my arrival and immediately made it clear I wasn't welcome.

"Bugger off, this is a private conversation," the blond one said as I approached.

It was Ed's new hero, Marty. I'd met him at the hospital but I hadn't hung around that day to pay him any attention. Close up now, he looked a bit older than us. His hair was cropped and his skin was pitted too. What was it with these footy guys? A flash of colour streaked out from his sleeve across his right bicep. A tat declaring love for his mum? Probably not: more likely, his name and address inked onto his bicep in case he forgot them. Still, he was a big bastard; I had to give him that.

Behind him Amy giggled – an odd manic sound – not like her at all.

My stomach cramped. This wasn't right. I tried to catch her eye but she refused to look at me.

"Yeah, get lost, Tommo. Go play more games with Casey," Lena hiccupped.

I finally spoke, doing my best to sound confident. "Leens, are you sure you don't want me to take you home? You're upset."

"I don't need you to take care of me, Tommo," she snapped, then downed her drink in one and turned to Amy who threw a protective arm around her.

Would they still be united tomorrow morning? Surely sober, Leens would realize that Amy was a devil woman?

"Of course she's upset. Your mate Casey's been pissing around with both of them. That's not cool, is it, Crazy?" Marty spoke with such authority I had to stop my head from nodding with Crazy's.

The guy I'd met earlier in the garden, whose name I still didn't know, added, "Yeah, but I reckon that Casey guy was just trying to convince everyone that he's not a fag like his brother."

I spun around to look at the girls. So they knew about Mikey. Amy was laughing but there was still something false about the sound. Leens didn't seem to be registering anything. She was slumped on the bench clinging to her now empty glass. Her eyes were almost shut and she was definitely oblivious to the fact that her spread legs had allowed her dress to ride up her thighs. She still looked hot. Marty seemed to be signalling to his mates with his eyes. I didn't need to speak Bomber to know what they were thinking.

Crazy grabbed the wine cask and headed over to top up Lena's glass. "More goon, Lena?" She opened her eyes and made a little protest but he filled her glass to the brim. She gulped from it at once to stop it spilling onto her legs and giggled. Then Crazy pulled her to her feet and began to spin her round. The wine sprayed everywhere as they danced back near the entrance where Mr No Name was standing.

I joined Amy who was now sitting on the edge of the bench, her body stiff and alert. Her eyes caught mine and grew wider as Marty followed the dancers and cut in. Now he was the one holding Leens. I guess we'd just witnessed a Bombers' set move.

Amy jumped to her feet but she seemed uncertain about what to do next. She turned to me.

I rolled my shoulders as if to say, "Not my problem. You got yourselves into this, remember?" But I didn't feel smug and she looked scared. Should I do something? Create a diversion of some sort? There was no point asking these guys to let the girls go. I was nothing to them. Our only connection was Ed. My brain raced. Mentioning Ed right now might just work.

I headed over to them, concentrating on keeping my voice steady. "Hey, Marty, I'm a bit worried about Ed. You guys should come and take a look at him. He's a bit out of it."

I got his attention but he didn't let go of Leens.

"What's wrong with little Eddy?" Crazy asked.

"He's lying back there somewhere asleep. I was just on my way to get someone to give me a hand to move him."

They looked at me as if I was mad. "He'll be right. He's just had too much, that's all."

"Too much what?"

They threw each other sneaky smiles instead of answering me. I tried again.

"Probably shouldn't leave him there, though. Can you guys help me get him inside?"

Marty shook his head. "You've got to be joking, mate. I've got my hands full at the moment." Without warning he grabbed Lena's right boob and squeezed it roughly. She gasped in shock. His friends screamed in drunken laughter. Amy froze.

"Oh, come on, don't be like that, Lena," he told her, releasing his grip slightly. "You've been wasting your time with that loser, Casey, for too long. We'll show you how it should be, won't we, Crazy?"

There was no ignoring Crazy's excited panting now as he watched Marty stroke Lena's arm. She managed to pull away to stand with Amy who was beside me now.

"Actually, Tommo, I think we will come and give you a hand with Ed," Amy said, dragging Lena with her. She seemed to have sobered up quickly. I moved to allow them to go ahead of me, but as I did, Marty sprang in front of them. Amy tried to sidestep him and failed.

"You don't need any help, do you, Tommy?" He spoke without looking at me.

The nerves that had been gurgling away in my stomach bubbled into my mouth. I felt sick. But I took too long to answer and jumped as I felt a hand on my shoulder. In an instant, I was being shoved by Crazy. I went toppling back into a huge rosebush and was immediately ensnared by thorns. I heaved myself up, tearing my shirt as I struggled to pull free. The metallic taste of blood filled my mouth just before the stinging kicked in. I'd ripped my top lip on a thorn. I dragged myself up and took a few steps forward but the third guy blocked my way now. The girls were sandwiched in between him and Marty.

"See you later, mate," Marty said, grabbing Lena roughly in a bear hug.

She began slapping at his arms. "Get off me!" But it only made him laugh.

"Come on, Lena, it's a party. Lighten up and we'll show you a good time."

"Let her go," Amy ordered, right before No Name grabbed her from behind.

"Fuck off!" Amy spun round and kicked him hard on the shin.

"You stupid bitch!" His hand snaked out and slapped her cheek. She gasped in shock. Or maybe I did. Silence descended for a few seconds until Marty broke it.

"Don't worry, Lena, unlike Robbie, I never hit chicks I want to root." He gave Lena another squeeze.

Behind them Amy was frozen.

"You'd have to pay me to do this moll," said Robbie as he bent down to rub his shin.

"Crazy will take her then, won't you?"

Lena turned to me with urgent eyes. I looked down at my feet. What did she expect me to do? These guys were mental and it was three against one. Did she think I was going to get my head kicked in for two girls who twenty minutes ago had hated my guts?

Marty scooped Lena up and, ignoring her screams, carried her back along the narrow path to the soft grass beyond the bench. He set her down on her feet, but she crumbled under his weight and hit the grass. Then he joined her.

"Tommo!" Amy had come to life again.

I took a step towards the struggling couple but was blocked by Robbie. I knew I'd have to go through him so I sucked up as much air as I could and surged forward, aiming my whole body at his massive chest. We staggered back on the path but he lost his footing and hit the deck, taking me with him. I wasn't on top for long. In another Bombers set move, I was flicked and turned and found myself fending off Robbie's punches and Crazy's kicks.

I registered each blow with gritted teeth, lashing out as hard as I could.

"Get off!" For a second I thought the cry had come from me until it was followed by another terrified scream – Amy!

I struggled to sit up and used all my strength to push Robbie away. As Crazy sank his foot into my thigh, I yanked it hard. He lost his balance and fell on top of Robbie. I jumped up and raced over to the grass, knowing I only had a few seconds before Dumb and Dumber caught up.

Lena was trapped under Marty's weight. Her eyes were

wide with panic. He had one massive hand clamped over her mouth and he was using the other to lash out at Amy as she kicked him. He was laughing wildly. I grabbed his shoulders and pulled but I could see it was hopeless because this was what he did best. He was a professional footy player. He was used to hanging on while blokes a lot heavier and meaner than Amy and I tried to rip his limbs off.

I let go as Crazy and Robbie arrived. Just before they jumped me I made a desperate attempt to get Marty's attention.

"Hey, Lena, don't worry about Marty. Apparently he's got such a small dick, you won't even know he's been there," I yelled.

They were on me at once.

Two or three?

"I read it in the paper," I shouted. "A whole heap of women have been complaining."

I couldn't get another word out, as someone smacked my mouth hard. Shit, it hurt. Had my plan worked? It was hard to tell in the flurry of fists and I have to confess by now my eyes were shut tight.

"You fucking little prick." Marty's sour breath in my face heralded a massive punch to my balls.

For a blissful second there was nothing, then agony ordered the contents of my guts to get the hell out. I heaved at least twice before I got onto my knees to do it properly. I couldn't see the girls anywhere. They must have taken off. My attackers backed away. Tears welled in my eyes and even though I was gasping in between vomits, my swollen lips curved into a secret grin. Clearly the irony of Marty's words was wasted on him. If being a dumb arse was an Olympic event, these three would be on the podium. I decided then that I was not going to die here.

I faked the next retch and dragged my body to a standing position, holding out a warning hand to them and teetering a bit as if I was about to projectile vomit. They hovered at a wider distance because none of them wanted to wear my spew. I pretended to stagger some more and when I judged they'd backed off far enough, I suddenly bolted in the opposite direction.

"YOU FU—" They chased me but the beer had slowed their reflexes. I was way too quick to hear the rest. My heart pumped pain relief into my body and I sprinted faster than I ever have towards Ed. If they did catch up with me, maybe he would be able to intervene. It was my only option.

31

I almost toppled over Ed in the end because he'd moved from where I'd left him. He was lying on his back with his eyes closed, but he wasn't still like before. I checked behind me for the Bombers but no one came. I dropped down beside him. He was grinding his teeth.

"Ed?" I put my bruised hand on his forehead. It was sizzling. "ED!" He opened his eyes and in the dim light I could tell that his pupils were huge and unseeing.

"Ed." I struggled to get him to his feet but he was a dead weight and in my beaten state, I could hardly even get his shoulders off the grass. My face throbbed. I wanted to crawl home but instead I grabbed his wrist and searched for a pulse. I couldn't locate one.

All thoughts of my own agonies disappeared.

Think, Tommo. Think.

I pressed my fingers deep into the side of his neck and found what I was looking for. I don't know how I'd missed it before: it was racing.

"Ed, can you hear me?" I shook him. Nothing.

This was serious now. I knew I had to get help, but I couldn't leave him like this. I struggled to remember the CPR stuff we'd done in Nippers all those years ago. He was obviously breathing so I didn't have to do all that kissing and pumping, but what else? There was something else.

And eventually it came back to me: recovery position and airway. I rolled him onto his side as fast as I could, bent his knee up and straightened his arm. Then I tilted his head back, waited for his teeth to stop gnashing for a second and stuck my fingers in his mouth. It was clear.

I rocked back on my heels, wiped my fingers on my jeans and considered what to do next. If I could get him out of here and back home, he'd probably be OK but there was no chance of me moving him when he was like this. I needed Casey. He should be here sharing the load.

Selfish prick!

I could go back to the house for help but what if I ran into Marty and his crew again? Who knew how many of the other gatecrashers up there had come with them? There was no point in calling Ed's mum on his phone when she was so far away and while I could call my own mum, that was definitely a last resort.

Ed groaned and I put my hand on his arm. Heat radiated through his T-shirt, despite the chill in the air. I watched him anxiously, waiting for him to do something else, but he didn't. I sighed in relief. I could cope with him lying there, groaning a bit.

But Ed has always been a contrary bastard and, as soon as I took my hand off him to check the time on my mobile, he started to shake violently.

What the hell had he taken? Not just alcohol. I knew I should be calling an ambulance, yet still I hesitated. If an ambulance came, would the police come too? How would they know? Would emergency services automatically call them? If the cops came, we'd all be in the shit. They would then check everything out at the house and who knows what they'd find.

I put my hands back on Ed and tried to hold him still. "Ed!" I yelled through my split lip, but he was totally out of it. Even if it was just paramedics who came, everyone in Rhona's street would see them. Would her neighbours then call the cops anyway? And I'd probably have to go in the ambulance with Ed. And once we got to the hospital, they'd contact his parents and after that I probably couldn't keep Mum from finding out. She'd crack it when she knew drugs were involved.

I shifted to get more comfortable. My back was killing me from where I'd been kicked. Ed seemed to be a bit calmer. Maybe the worst of it was over. Maybe I could leave him and he would just sleep it off and no one would ever know.

"Ed?" I tried again to wake him, fighting the urge to thump him in sheer frustration.

Why me? Why not his new footy mates? He took his chances when he had whatever it was they gave him, he should have to wear that now. I mean, it's not as if I didn't try to give him a heads-up about this stuff before.

I opted to stand up. It felt good to make a decision about something.

"Ed," I shouted, nudging him with my foot. Still nothing. That's when I heard a sound behind me. My heart sank. Had Marty found me? I spun round and to my relief it was Casey. He looked as surprised to see me as I did to see him.

"What are you doing here?" he slurred.

I stood aside so he could see Ed.

"What happened to him?"

"I dunno. He's taken some shit that those Bombers guys gave him. He's in a bad way. We need to do something."

He shrugged. "Not my problem."

"What?"

He didn't answer and began to walk away.

"Where are you going?"

"Home," he said. "There's a back way out over that wall down there. I'll tell you something, Tommo, I'm bloody sick of women. They're all bitches. Do you know what Rhona said to—?"

"I don't give a shit what Rhona said, Casey! Take a look at Ed. He needs help."

"We all need help, mate." He swayed on his feet. "I need help but I don't see anyone queuing up."

"Are you for real?"

He held up an unsteady hand. "Hey, I've got problems—"

"Yeah, and they're all because you can't keep your dick in your pants," I snapped.

"Nah, it's not just about Lena and Rhona and…"

"And Amy. What is it about, Casey? How can anybody help you when you won't tell us what's going on? You can't still be pissed about Mikey? Get over it. You're not the first guy in the world whose brother's gay." I was finding it hard to yell because my lips had started to scab over and they felt tight. A trickle of blood ran down my chin.

Casey noticed it. "What happened to you?"

"Believe it or not, I've got problems too. I've just had the shit kicked out of me by Ed's mates."

He started to smirk.

"They practically raped Lena and Amy!" I shouted.

He shrugged. "Those two chicks can look after themselves. Trust me."

"Are you kidding me? You weren't there. And the only reason they were in any danger was because you messed with their heads in the first place. In fact—"

"Spare me the bullshit, Tommo. Yeah, I'm a bastard and you're a hero. You might even be able to crack onto one of them now, so you should be thanking me."

A hot surge of rage propelled me forwards. I crash tackled him to the ground.

"What are you doing?" he screamed as I punched him hard in the stomach. He threw a couple of stray fists back but he was too disorientated for them to do much damage. My whole body ached but I found the strength to thump him again. His lip split. I enjoyed that.

"You WANKER!" He tried to roll me onto my back. Just as I grabbed his T-shirt to distribute my weight, a sickening gurgling sound filled the air. At first I thought it was Casey but he'd stopped struggling. "What's that?"

I crawled off him and over to Ed. He was vomiting and shaking violently. I heaved him onto his side then I whipped out my mobile and began to dial.

"What are you doing?" Casey asked.

"He needs an ambulance."

Casey stood up, took a look at Ed and turned away.

"Casey, we need to wait with him!"

"He's got you, he doesn't need me," he said, without looking back.

"Casey, you can't—" I didn't get to finish because the voice on the line was asking me questions. While I was answering them, Casey disappeared into the night.

It took seconds to pass on the necessary information; just seconds to blow our lives apart and after I'd done it, I knelt helplessly beside my mate, praying for sirens.

32

When Dad was in hospital a few years ago with some mysterious virus that attacked his heart, I remember dreading having to visit him. It had made me feel ill. At one point I'd tried to beg out of going.

"I can't stand hospitals, Mum. Can't you just go without me?"

"Don't be ridiculous," she'd snapped and ordered me to the car. That was the end of that. I don't know that hating hospitals is ridiculous, but I guess using it as an excuse not to visit someone is. Basically, it's selfish.

Sitting there waiting for the word on Ed, I was on the verge of being very selfish. Whenever the automatic doors opened and some bleeding body blundered in, I wanted to run. It didn't help that every time the frantic nurses bustled past, they still had time to scowl at me as if I was public enemy number one. They were obviously holding me responsible for Ed's condition.

The paramedics had been far too busy to be judgemental

when they'd arrived at Rhona's. By then we had a bit of an audience as some people had followed the lights down to the bottom of the garden. I noticed Kieran but I couldn't see Amy or Leens. No one spoke to me and as the paramedics started asking stuff, people moved off. No one wants to be asked those kind of questions at a party.

"What's your mate taken?" The older medic asked.

"Dunno."

"Has he been drinking?"

I shrugged.

"Come on, son, we're not the cops and we're not your parents. Just tell us what you know."

"Beer, I suppose … and maybe vodka."

He told me a few weeks ago he'd tried vodka. "It's great, Tommo. It gets you off your face but no one can smell it on your breath."

I looked down at him. There wasn't much breath coming from him now.

"Has he smoked or inhaled anything? Has he taken any tablets?"

"I don't know. I don't know!" I lashed out at a can that one of the recent onlookers had dropped. My kick sent it sailing into the air and liquid sprayed the ground in an arc.

The younger medic put his hand on my arm while his partner worked busily on Ed. "Settle down, son. If there's nothing else you can tell us about your mate, that's OK."

His words spun in my head. There was lots more I could tell them about my mate: he was great at footy, shit at Maths, mad about chicks, hated the news, loved *The Simpsons* and he was a really funny guy, but I couldn't tell them anything that might save his life. I guess I didn't know him well enough any more.

They put him on a stretcher and carried him into the waiting ambulance.

Then the young guy called to me, "Are you OK, or do you need help too?"

"What do you mean?"

He pointed to my face. "Doesn't look too good."

"I'm fine."

"Well, jump in and let's get going."

I did what I was told and they slammed the doors shut.

When I was a little kid I always wanted to ride in an ambulance with the lights and the noise clearing the way. That night I would have given anything to be somewhere else.

In contrast to the urgency of the sirens and the beating of my heart, Ed was totally still. His grey face was covered by a clear plastic mask and although they'd attempted to wrap him in a blanket, I could see where they'd ripped his shirt to attach wires to his chest.

Unable to bear looking at him, I angled myself so that I could stare out of the windscreen between their two seats. The driver flicked on the siren and we rumbled across the lawn and out the back way.

As we waited briefly in the driveway while cars slowed down to let us out, the headlights picked out a figure standing directly opposite Rhona's garden. It was Casey. He watched us turn onto the road. I hated him then.

At one point on the short journey the older guy shouted into the back, "Have you taken anything yourself, mate?"

I shook my head and found myself saying, "It wasn't me. I didn't give him the stuff, I just found him."

He didn't even bother turning round when he said, "Nothing to do with us, mate."

When we arrived at the Emergency ward they bundled Ed in through the doors to the waiting medics. I stood in the cool night air wondering what to do next. It made sense to get the hell out of there. I'd got him where he needed to be and if I hung around any longer, I would probably end up in the shit too.

Before I could decide a nurse appeared. "Are you the boy who arrived with the overdose patient?" She gave a little shiver as she looked at me.

Overdose? My head swam. Was he dead? I tried to ask but the words wouldn't come out.

"Well, are you?"

I nodded lamely.

"Are you related?"

I shook my head.

"We need to know some of his details. Come inside and we'll give you a form."

I followed her into the warmth of the hospital waiting room.

"Is he going to be OK?"

"Someone will talk to you about him soon." She smiled before she left.

That had been nearly two hours ago. I shifted for the millionth time in the orange plastic chair. At least I was in the right place to have it surgically removed from my arse when I finally got out of there. I looked across at the triage desk only to catch another nurse scowl in my direction. I felt my face burn with indignation. I held it in my hands and stayed like that for a while before becoming aware of footsteps. They stopped in front of me.

"Are you with Edward Saunders?"

I found myself looking at a female doctor. She seemed much younger than she probably was, considering how long doctors spend at uni. She was hot but there was something weird about her eyes and it wasn't just that they looked tired. I missed what she was saying at first because I was trying to work it out. Finally I did. One was green and the other was a sort of blue-grey. I've never seen anyone with odd-coloured eyes before.

"...contact?" She was clearly expecting an answer.

"Sorry?"

"I said we need an adult contact." My heart sank.

"Is it bad?"

She looked at me like I was an idiot then she spoke very slowly to make sure I understood her. "I – just – told – you – we've – managed – to – stabilize – him for the time being but we must get his parents here. He wasn't making much sense when we tried to talk to him before but he seems to think there's no way we can reach them, would that be right?"

"He doesn't see his dad and his mum is up the coast at his gran's place."

"Do you have a contact number for her?"

"It should be in his phone."

"He doesn't have one on him."

"Can't you just ask him for her number?"

She shook her head.

"Why not?"

"He's not conscious."

I rubbed my neck. It felt stiff as. "Can't you just wait until the morning?"

"We probably could, but the police won't and they're on their way."

My mouth went dry.

"Duty of care. We have to report all cases of illegal drug use when minors are involved," she told me. "And they want to talk to you too." As if she was reading my mind, she added, "You gave us all your details when you brought him in here, so there's no point in disappearing." She turned to leave and then said, "I'll have someone take a look at your lip later."

I slumped back into the hard orange chair as she moved off, feeling sick. I was way out of my depth here. There was only one thing to do. Ignoring the signs about mobile phones, I keyed in a number with trembling fingers. She answered on the second ring.

"Mum, I'm in trouble." And I'm not proud to say I burst into tears.

33

In the end, the cops went pretty easy on me but I don't know if that was down to Mum towering over them in her scarlet Jimmy Choos or not. She arrived just after they did and both officers stood up at the same time to offer her a seat. She rewarded their chivalry with a radiant smile, chose the chair to my right and put her arm around my shoulders. The lump that I'd banished in the presence of the cops came rushing back into my throat.

"My God, are you OK?" She reached out to my face.

"It probably looks worse than it is," I lied and nestled into her neck. She cupped the swollen side of my face in her left hand as she looked up at the police officers.

"Charlotte Sweeney." She held out her right hand without getting up and they both tripped over themselves to shake it. "Let's get on with this, shall we?"

We all did as she commanded. They asked a lot of questions and I tried to answer them without dobbing on anyone. It wasn't easy.

"And this fight that you were in wasn't connected to Edward Saunders?"

"Not really."

"And you don't want to report it?"

"No." I was expecting Mum to protest but she didn't interrupt.

"Did you take anything yourself, mate?"

"No."

"What about alcohol?"

I hesitated a fraction too long.

"How much, Tommy?" Mum asked.

"Just a few beers."

"No tablets?" The cop pressed. "Did you smoke anything?"

"No." I was prompt with that answer and Mum let out a little sigh of relief.

They asked more questions about Ed, his mates and his mum and finally they said we could go. Mum stood first, holding out her hand. I grabbed it like a kindy kid.

"We'll just need you to come to the station on Monday and sign a statement, please."

"We'll do that, officer," Mum told him.

The older of the two patted my shoulder. "You did the right thing, son."

She demanded an explanation about my face as soon as we escaped the police that night. I guess I was in the mood to be absolutely honest.

She looked ill when I'd finished. "Were these girls in serious danger?"

"I think so but I can't be sure now."

And I couldn't. It was as though the scene in the garden was something I'd watched on TV and not lived. Scary as it was at the time, everything that happened afterwards had been much worse. Who knows how it would have played out? Maybe Marty was just pushing his luck a bit too far and would have come to his senses.

"So you don't think we should report these boys?"

"No! That's up to Lena and Amy. And I've just told the police that I don't want anyone charged."

We'd reached home by then so she let it go. It was close to 3 a.m. but she ran me a bath, which I soaked in for a while, fighting sleep.

I didn't get out of bed until three on Sunday. I spent the rest of the afternoon moping around the house, nursing my wounds. My bones ached but not as much as my ears. Mum lectured me constantly about underage drinking and drug taking and I wore it knowing I would get some peace the next day when she went to work.

Sucked in me. She worked at home on the Monday after we'd been to sign my statement and seemed to be beside me whenever I made a move. She even cooked on Monday night. I was astonished.

"The launch is on Wednesday, so I have to go in tomorrow," she said over tuna baked potatoes.

"Should I try calling the hospital again?" I asked.

"I don't think so. You're becoming a nuisance caller, Tommy."

"But they never seem to tell me anything."

"That's because there's nothing to tell. He's stable and responding to treatment and I'm sure if there's any change his mum will call us."

I sighed.

"I think you should go back to school tomorrow."

"But I…"

"I know." She glanced at my bruised face. "You're mad at Casey but you'll have to face him eventually."

I ignored that. "Everyone will probably hate me for wrecking the party. They all know I was the one who called the ambulance."

"You had no choice. They'll understand that. Ed could have died. He had a very severe reaction to those drugs."

"I suppose."

"This is the kind of thing that you kids don't get about binge drinking," she said, pouring herself a white wine in a glass the size of a bucket.

Oh, no, she was about to go off again.

"You kids think you're invincible. You don't stop to consider for a minute that it could all go horribly wrong in a few seconds. Bad things happen to good people, Tommy."

"I know," I said.

"No, you don't and it scares me to death. Imagine if things had gone too far in that garden on Saturday night? All your lives would have changed forever, even this Marty character's. He may seem old to you but, believe me, he's just a kid too. Imagine going from being a promising footballer to a rapist in the blink of an eye just because he substanced himself senseless? Or imagine if they had severely injured you and you'd ended up with brain damage or something?"

Substanced himself senseless? She'd invented a new word.

"What are you grinning at?"

"Nothing."

"Well, it's nice to see a smile on your face at last," she said.

"I've had a really bad couple of weeks."

"Do you want to tell me about it?"

I did. I told her about Mikey being gay and the Caseys' shock split and Ed's new mates. I told her about Casey cheating on Leens and Amy and Rhona, and I told her I'd liked both Leens and Amy but that I'd blown my chances there.

"You never know. They might come round in the end. You did rescue them after all."

I wasn't so sure.

"And what about Steven Casey? How do you feel about him now?"

"Angry. Angry like I could smash his face in again."

Mum smiled gently. "That's understandable."

"No, you don't get it. I really hate him."

"It's always painful when friends betray you. Steven stuffed up but you shouldn't hate him for it."

"Are you taking his side? Do you think it was OK for him to be a selfish prick and let everybody down?"

She didn't even flinch at my language. Instead, she sipped her wine and took a long moment to respond. She does this a lot these days when we're arguing. It makes me feel even madder … but also kind of stupid at the same time.

"I wasn't aware that this was about taking sides," she said. "If it is, I take yours."

I felt stupid.

"I think the problem is that you guys just don't know each other as much as you think you do. In fact, you probably don't know yourselves either."

I looked up and she smiled. "You should work on that. Self-knowledge is like having a…" She frowned as she searched for the right words. "Raincoat for stormy days."

I expected more but she just stopped talking, and sat back in her chair.

"I hope things don't get any stormier than this."

She rolled her eyes. "Hey, speak to me when you've got a mortgage to choke on, a job that no one does as well as you and a kid who pulls you away from a free Strawberry Daiquiri to sweet-talk a couple of cops!"

I was so relaxed chatting with Mum, I thought about fessing up to being Carrie Edwards but I didn't: no point in pushing my luck.

I moved the tuna around my dinner plate (it's hard to imagine someone stuffing up canned fish but somehow Mum had managed it), and added, "I think I get what you're saying, but they're supposed to be my best mates and now I feel like I don't even know them. Maybe it's just over."

"Well, if it is, it would be a pity to part hating each other after all these years."

"I know, but I can't help the way I feel."

"Perhaps you can have a different type of friendship now. Different is not necessarily worse."

"What do you mean?"

"One where you don't live in each others' pockets so much." Her chair scraped back. "Come on, help me clear up."

Later we watched some TV but all the time her words were spiders' webs snarling up thoughts of Casey. He hadn't phoned once since our fight, not even to see how Ed was. I got what Mum was trying to say, I really did, but afterwards in the blackness of another sleepless night, I still wanted to smash his face in!

34

I slipped back into school on Tuesday without any fuss. No one accused me of wrecking the party but then again, no one was thanking me either.

The word was out that Ed was finally home and as far as the truth goes, that was it. The rest was all rumour.

"Ed Saunders is a steroid junkie."

"Ed Saunders had to be resuscitated in the ambulance."

"Ed Saunders tried to kill himself."

"Ed Saunders has lost his contract with the Bombers."

That last one shocked me. Could it be true? How would the Bombers' management have found out? It's not as if Marty would have told them and surely even Crazy wasn't that crazy?

There was no sign of Ed or Casey but I spotted Amy and Lena during recess. They pretended they didn't see me. That pissed me off. They seemed to have conveniently forgotten about the fact that I'd volunteered to be the Bombers' punching bag to help them out. I didn't really give a stuff about

Amy but I figured my friendship with Leens could be worth saving. I got out my phone. It took me ages to come up with my text.

Hi. How R U? Sorry about U & Casey. Sorry about wot happened in the garden. Tommo x.

I waited years on her reply and when it came, I found my finger trembling as I pushed the button.

Thanx.

Was that it?

I tried again.

Do U want to catch up after school?

My phone beeped. *Not a good idea.*

Why wasn't it a good idea?

I tried again. *Why not? R U mad at me?*

The response wasn't so fast this time but it did finally arrive. *No, I'm mad at me.*

My thumb flew over the keypad. *Don't get what you mean.*

Again, there was at least a three-minute delay before she answered. *Don't worry. Just need some space. Speak later.*

It was better than nothing. I wondered why she was mad at herself. Was it for not realizing what Casey was up to? Or was it for getting wasted and stuck in the garden with the Bombers? That was pretty dumb but Amy did it too. I didn't think there was much chance of Amy being mad at herself. Poor Leens. I decided to give it a couple of days and if I didn't hear from her I'd try again.

I headed up the stairs for lesson three and turned into the first floor corridor. The window-lined wall overlooks the car park and as I glanced out, a car pulled in. I recognized it immediately. Mr C was dropping Casey off. He stayed double-parked while I continued to watch, expecting Casey to get out at any moment. I was glad to have the chance to see him first without him seeing me.

He took ages to come out and, for a moment, I wondered if he could see me. Impossible from this angle. My eyes bored into the car and I wished it had one of those sunroofs so I could see inside. The back window looked a bit foggy. Obviously, there was no way I could hear a thing but I had a feeling they were arguing in there.

Eventually, the passenger door opened and Casey appeared. His face was pale but there were two spots of colour on his cheeks. He took a step away from the car and seemed to change his mind because he leaned back in again. I couldn't see his head but his shoulders were rigid. I was certain he was giving Mr C a serve. As his head came back into view his bag came hurtling out of the passenger seat, narrowly missing him. His books scattered everywhere. He stooped down to pick them up and there was no doubt from his contorted face that he was yelling again. He didn't lean in this time. He finished shouting and headed for the student entrance without closing the car door.

Mr C got out and stomped round the car to the passenger seat. He slammed the door so hard the whole car rocked. Then he turned and yelled something at Casey's retreating back. Casey stopped dead in his tracks, turned and gave him the finger. Mr C yelled something else, got back in and skidded away like a P-plater showing off.

I watched the exhaust smoke slowly disappear. What the hell was going on?

Realizing I was now seriously late for class I made a move, but as I did, I heard footsteps in the stairwell. I knew it was him. I turned expectantly to the door just as Casey came through. His eyes met mine and, for a second, I thought he was going to bolt off.

"What was that all about?" I said, nodding in the direction of the car park.

He glared at me. "None of your business."

For a moment we were two silent, seething statues.

"Aren't you going to say anything about Saturday night?" I said, finally giving in.

"Shit party."

"You're joking, aren't you? Is that all you can come up with? Don't you even want to know how Ed is?"

"He's fine. I told you he would be." He pretended to fish for something in his bag.

"It's no thanks to you he's fine," I reminded him.

He looked up with a smirk. "What do you want, hero boy? A medal?"

"Get fucked, Casey!" It was only the start of what I needed to tell him.

"As you've just seen, mate, I already am."

If he wanted pity, he was talking to the wrong person.

"You're not the only one around here with shit going on. You're just the one who causes it." My voice was rising. "You're a selfish bastard."

I thought I saw a flicker of the old Casey, but then it died. He shrugged and said nothing.

I realized in that second that our friendship was over. The sad thing was I knew I could handle it. Somewhere down the corridor a door opened and Mr Day stuck his head out.

"Oi, get to class, you two."

We ignored him and stared at each other. I studied Casey's face closely. Couldn't tell what the hell he was thinking. He'd changed so much this year and yet he looked exactly the same. He still had the little scar above his left eyebrow where Ed had hit him with a stick-sword when we were six; the slightly uneven nose, which I'd broken with a cricket ball when we were eleven; and the zit-free skin that Ed and I envied.

Mr Day was waiting on an answer. "Guys?" His voice echoed.

Suddenly Casey spoke. "Just leave it, Tommo." He turned, walked past Mr Day as if he didn't exist and disappeared into room seventeen.

I left it. What else could I do?

35

I played the scene with Casey over in my head for most of the night and pretty much all of the next morning.

He wasn't at school and neither was Ed, who still hadn't even bothered to call me. I stormed into English and got through most of the lesson without taking in a word until Mrs Lennon said, "What do you think, Tom?"

"Dunno, I wasn't listening." Obviously, I had a death wish today. I was sure my response would annoy her but it didn't.

"We're talking about self-loathing. A couple of the girls have raised the point that in the DVD version of the book, Wickham seems to suffer from it at times, especially when he's hiding in London with Lydia."

I gulped. Who was hiding in London? The whole class was looking at me now. Among the sea of faces my eyes anchored on Amy's. She held my gaze and, to my amazement, a very tiny smile began to form.

"I disagree," she said and Mrs Lennon turned to her. "I think Mr Wickham's incapable of self-loathing. I think that's a quality that can only be felt by people who are truly prepared to be critical of their own actions and I don't think everyone is capable of that."

"You could be right, Amy. Does anyone want to add to Amy's comments?"

Carla joined the debate. "But couldn't you argue that if you … like … absolutely hate yourself … even though you know you're being like this totally uncool person, you just can't stop yourself … because you want to keep hating yourself? It's like a big circle." She giggled.

Dunno what she'd said that was so good but Amy and Miss were looking at her as if she was a genius. Then Amy looked back at me. The smile was replaced this time by a weird look, as if she was trying to communicate some urgent message but I didn't get it. What had Mr Wickham got to do with anything? Just then the bell went and as I walked past the teacher's desk, Mrs Lennon said, "I hear you had a busy weekend, Tom."

Instinctively, I checked to see who was around. Amy was still at her desk, frantically copying some notes about Mr Wickham from the board and Carla was fluffing around with her bag.

"Yeah, my dance card was pretty full, Miss."

She chuckled. "Do you know something, Tom? From what I hear, not even the accomplished Mr Darcy could have handled your situation any better. Integrity is an underrated quality nowadays."

"Maybe that's because nobody really knows what it means," I offered.

She peered at me over the top of her glasses. "Oh, I think you do." She dismissed me with a wink.

I felt as though I'd just found a blazing fire on the face of a glacier. Her words thawed every numb part of me and I felt warm again for the first time in days. Sure, it's one thing for your parents to reassure you you've done the right thing, but no one else had and I realized then that this was a big part of the problem. It was like Saturday night just hadn't happened. Everyone seemed to be moving on as normal except for me, Casey and Ed. Our lives had frozen in time that night. I gave her a final glance but she'd already turned her attention back to her laptop.

I moved to the doorway at exactly the same time as Carla and jumped back to let her through. I've seen her suddenly stop in doorways for no reason a million times before and I wasn't risking thumping into her this time. My bones were still too sore from Saturday night.

"Thanks, Tommo."

"No worries," I muttered.

She paused, made an effort to harness her thoughts and said, "I heard what you did on the weekend. It must have been hard." She gave me a brief smile and glided off before I could respond. I don't know what surprised me more, her words of support, or the fact that up close she had the most gorgeous green eyes I've ever seen.

Recovering myself, I made a second attempt to get through the door at the same time as Amy.

"Sorry," I said and braced myself for the barrage of abuse

that would probably follow. She took the longest time to answer but all she said in the end was, "Me too."

She held my gaze with a disturbing intensity and we stood there drinking each other in, unable to utter another word.

"Get to class, please." Mrs Lennon broke the spell. Amy shot through the door, leaving me gaping.

36

"I'll be late tonight," Mum said on Thursday morning. "Got to pick Dad up from the airport at 7 p.m. and we're going out for dinner." We were both wearing stupid smiles. Somehow Dad's return marked an end of the chaos, but neither of us voiced the thought. Her launch had gone without a hitch the day before and she was relaxed and happy.

If Ed or Casey were in, I didn't see them in the yard that morning. At some point, I remembered that I had to deal with the Carrie Edwards thing for Mum. She was already in trouble there because I'd missed the Monday deadline for the last two problems. It was probably for the best. The only way out now was to get her fired. All I had to do was sign into Ed's account with his password and reply to the last two problems in the most random way possible and ignore today's new ones. Easy!

That's exactly what I was doing at lunch when I saw Casey again.

"Are you still messing around with that problem thing?" he

asked, pulling up a chair. "Thought you said you were getting out of it?"

I didn't know what to say. It was surreal. Was he really going to pretend that nothing had happened? Could I? I found myself responding. "Yeah, I'm trying to get fired."

There were several emails from Mum marked "Urgent". No doubt she was panicking about Carrie's late replies. I didn't open any of them.

"Have you seen Lena recently?" he asked suddenly.

"No. Why would I see her?"

He shrugged. "Just wondered."

Was I was being accused of something? "Look, I wasn't trying to crack on to Leens, if that's what you think. I just needed her help with the column."

"Don't worry about it. She wasn't getting much attention from me."

"As if anyone was."

"I've had a lot going on." His tone took me by surprise. For the first time in ages I couldn't hear any hostility. It unnerved me.

"Your dad?" I felt I had to say something.

"Everyone."

I waited, certain he was going to elaborate.

"Do you still want help with these problems?" He spun the monitor round before I could refuse. He read them quickly, then said, "Right, you want ridiculous?"

I nodded because I wasn't sure what else to do. Then I remembered something Lena said about Casey being too hard to talk to. She was right. It was like playing chess with words. I had the weirdest feeling one of us was about to be check-mated and I didn't want it to be me.

"OK, type this: *Dear Ali, forget volunteering. If you want to do a gap year, take the army up on their invite to do your gap year with them. They'll send you on a Contiki tour of a war zone. PS: Good luck at uni if you ever make it back.*"

I couldn't help myself, I laughed.

"And for the first one?" He read Mel's letter. "Just say, *Get over it, Mel. Lots of kids do.* OK?"

"Do they?" I asked as I typed.

To: edwards@mailwatch.com
From: charliesweeney@panpublications.com
Subject: Re: your column

Hi Charlie,

Sorry these responses are late.

Hope the launch went well.

Regards

Tommy.

By the time I'd finished, he still hadn't answered.

Eventually, he said, "Do you really want to know?"

To my amazement, despite everything, I realized I actually did. Checkmate. He'd got me.

I nodded and read over my reply to mum while he strug-gled to find his words. Bloody hell, I'd signed it with my own name instead of Carrie's. Just as I was about to fix it, Casey spoke. "Everything's different now and I can't handle it."

I turned to him. "Is this about Mikey?"

"No." Then he seemed to think about it. "Well, yeah, kind of."

I shifted in my seat. "Casey, you know the whole gay thing…?" but I didn't get to finish.

"No, it's not about that. It's more about secrets. You know? About your family not talking, not sharing anything."

I didn't know. "Maybe once all this Mikey stuff settles…" I tried.

He laughed, an odd scratching sound.

"It's always been shit at my place. It's always been one big performance. All those great sleepovers and the family breakfasts and dinners that were put on for you and Ed, with Mum and Dad chatting away … it was all a lie." He was spitting the words.

I was stunned. "What do you mean?"

"Do you think that's how our lives were when no one was around?"

He must have seen the horror on my face because he waved his hand. "No! We weren't abused or anything, it's nothing like that. Dad didn't hit us or slap Mum around. The weapon of choice in the Casey household has always been silence. Long days of it. Everyone living inside their own heads. Mum and Dad too numb to even hate each other in the end. But at least me and Mikey were always honest with each other. Then I found out that was a lie too."

For the first time in ages, I began to understand him.

"Mikey's news just brought things to a head, but what really pisses me off is that he drops his bomb from miles away and I'm stuck with the wreckage. Mum won't be back. I reckon she's wanted to go for a long time."

"You'll still see her though?"

"Suppose."

"Maybe your dad will come round if you talk."

"Are you for real? Now he's too pissed every night to talk even if he wanted to."

"Have you tried?"

"What's the point?"

"What about talking to Mikey?"

He shook his head. "Why should I? How can I trust him now that I know he has his secrets too? How can I be sure anyone really means what they say?"

I wanted to tell him about Ed meeting Mikey in the city. I was certain Mikey had only told everyone because he thought Ed would. In the end I decided against it. That was a conversation he and Ed needed to have.

"You need to talk to your dad, Casey. It's just you and him now. You need to give it a go."

He sighed and buried his head in his hands. My hand lurched away from me and hovered so close above his shoulders I could feel the heat from his body. I wanted to touch him. I moved my hand higher.

Slap! I smacked him on the head. "Get over it, you wanker!"

His neck snapped up. His eyes were blazing. Then he

grinned at me and we fell into an amicable silence, which I broke with a question.

"Why did you mess around on Leens?"

He looked down at his feet. "I feel shit about that now but it just happened. I can't explain it. It was fun at first and I guess I kept on doing it because I could. It made me feel…" he paused.

"Feel what?"

"Better."

"Yeah, you looked heaps better on Saturday night," I added.

We both laughed. It seemed to me like we'd come to some sort of crossroads. I wanted to choose the way but I couldn't – still too hurt, too wary, not sure I could trust him to follow – so I didn't speak.

"I shouldn't have left you with Ed. I hung around for a bit, you know? I waited across the road to see if an ambulance definitely came but I just couldn't go back. I was out of it."

"You should have called."

"I know. I fucked up but at least you didn't. I'm sorry … hero boy."

He hesitated before saying the last phrase and I think maybe it was because he was scared I'd take it the wrong way. I took it as the first step on the new path.

I know girls at this school who hug each other if they've been separated for one lesson. Casey and I had been apart for way longer. There was no way I could give him a hug in the middle of the computer room but I wanted to. A footy kind of hug, I mean. As if he was reading my mind, he thumped me on the back. I caught his hand and clung to it for a few seconds before we both let go and quickly checked out the room to make sure no one had seen us.

"It's OK," I said in a voice that was just too squeaky for my liking. I turned back to the emails in an effort to get a grip and clicked on the send button at exactly the same time as I remembered I'd forgotten to change my signature.

"FUCK!"

"What's wrong, mate?" Casey asked, the smile dying on his lips.

"I'm a dead man."

37

Her text came through about an hour later.

I'll be picking you up from school, Tommy, and as you're so good with answers lately, you better have some for me.

I shuddered. This was a nightmare. I couldn't believe how quickly things had turned bad again.

"Is there anything I can do?" Casey asked before last lesson.

I shook my head.

"Tell her we were all in it together."

"Somehow I don't think that will improve my chances of survival, mate."

"Maybe she'll go easy on you after the weekend and everything."

"I doubt that."

"I'm really sorry, Tommo. I just don't know what to do to help."

At the end of the day he stood with me, as I waited at the school gate for Mum. Her little black sports car sprinted up to the kerb. The top was down and her hair was loose and messy. That was a good sign. Could mean she was relaxed.

"She seems OK," Casey said.

I was about to agree when I realized something. "Yeah, but her stereo's off. Not in a mood for music? That's got to be trouble."

She came to a halt and snapped, "Get in," without even looking around.

"Hi, Mrs Sweeney," Casey called cheerfully. "I'll ring you later," he whispered as I left the safety of his side and walked the plank to the car.

We sped off in silence but my brain and I were arguing.

"Apologize! Get it in first before she speaks."

"Don't be stupid. Shut up and wait."

"You've got to at least appear to be sorry."

We came to a red light and she finally looked my way. It was impossible to see her eyes through her massive sunglasses, but her voice was tight.

"Why, Tommy?"

"I'm sorry, Mum. I really am. I just didn't think about what it might mean for you."

"Have you any idea what it does mean? We have just launched a magazine claiming to be relying on expert contributors and one of my experts is a bloody seventeen year old who's suddenly started behaving like a baby again."

Ouch!

"I know, and when I figured out how serious it could be, I tried to get out of it. That's why I wrote the really bad replies this time. I knew you'd have to sack her." Her head whipped around and the car swerved a little. "I mean, me."

"But why do it in the first place? I don't understand." The light turned green, but she didn't move.

"It was an accident. Drive," I added, just as she was beeped by the car behind.

"Oh, shut up!" she yelled. Don't know if she was talking to me, or the driver.

"How can you *accidentally* become an agony aunt for a girl's magazine, Tommy? And this answer better be bloody good."

So I told her the whole sorry saga. I even told her about how I made up problems to get Lena's attention. Did she seem to soften slightly at that or was that just wishful thinking? I don't know how my response measured up on her "bloody good" scale because she said nothing when I'd finished. We'd pulled up in our driveway by then. She got out quickly, grabbing her briefcase and marched inside, leaving me sitting there, which I did for some time.

When I went inside, her study door was closed and I could hear her talking on the phone. I took refuge in my bedroom until I knew it was time for her to pick Dad up, then I hung around the kitchen, hoping I'd get some hint about what was going to happen next.

She came in to grab her car keys. "I'm going to get Dad."

"OK."

"I'm late." She wasn't really.

"OK."

"And it's because I've spent hours on the phone to our lawyers at Pan Pacific. Apparently, this will require a lot of blind-eye turning that will make everyone feel very uncomfortable. I'm furious about this, Tommy. I'm so offended that you would place so little value on what I do to mess around with it the way you did."

I squirmed.

"You have no idea how much you have compromised me today."

"I'm sorry, Mum. I don't know how to make it up to you."

She reached into her handbag, pulled out a tiny gold mirror and began to inspect her lipstick.

"Tommy, I guarantee you will be under no illusion about how you are going to make this up to me when I have made that decision."

She snapped the mirror shut. I winced and looked away.

"You're going to be an expert in agony when I'm finished with you, Carrie Edwards."

I looked to see if she was smiling but she wasn't.

"Now get yourself something for dinner, please," she commanded, and left me standing there wondering if the worst had passed.

Later that night when Casey called, he too was undecided.

"All I can say is it's a good job your dad is coming home tonight. It's sure to take her mind off you."

I agreed.

"I cleaned up the house a bit when I got home," he said.

"We've let it get in a bit of a state. Dad's working late tonight but I told him we have to speak soon."

"That's a great start," I offered.

"Yeah. You heard from Ed yet?"

"Nah. His phone's missing."

"Is it? I guess that's why he's not answering."

We talked easily about random stuff for a bit before ending the call.

As I turned my light off around eleven, I heard my parents come home.

I strained my ears. Was that Mum laughing? Sounded like it. I figured they'd gone into the kitchen to make coffee but someone must have ducked out because I heard someone climbing the stairs. When my door opened a chink, I held my breath, ready to fake sleep if it was Mum.

I could tell from his weight as he crossed the room to sit on the end of my bed that it was Dad. I flicked on the light. He looked tired.

"Tommy?"

"Yeah, Dad?" I braced myself for the lecture, wishing I could just give him a hug to show him how much I'd missed him.

"It's only natural, you know."

"What is?"

"This confusion over your sexuality, mate."

"Eh?"

"Don't worry, you can come clean with me. I grant you, pretending to actually be a woman is a bit unusual, but we can get you some counselling for that. Just promise me you'll stay out of Mum's wardrobe until we do." He leaned across the bed and planted a kiss on my face before I had time to reply. As I held on to him, we both laughed.

"Is she still mad?"

"Of course. You were way out of line with this stunt."

"I know."

"I'm not taking your side in this one, mate, even if the fall-out lasts for a couple of weeks. You deserve it."

"I know."

"Your mother works too bloody hard for you to compromise her like that."

"I know," I almost wailed.

"I haven't even compromised your mother like that." He smiled. "Keep your head down for a few days. She'll come round." He got up to leave.

"Dad."

"Yeah?"

"I'm glad you're home."

"I bet you are."

He gave me a wink and turned off my light.

38

On Friday Casey and I were having lunch in the gym when Ed materialized out of nowhere.

"You right?" he asked, dropping onto the bench beside us. Casey shot me a look but I wasn't sure what it meant.

"So where are we on the Carrie Edwards thing?" I couldn't believe he was acting like nothing had happened. Cool, I'd play his game too.

"It's over." I told him about the latest developments.

Before he had time to respond, Casey asked, "So where are we on the drug overdose thing?" He picked a stray piece of lettuce off his lap and put it back into his lunch bag.

There was a brief pause before Ed sniffed and asked, "So where are we on the screwing three girls at the same time?"

"I was not screwing them," Casey exploded.

"You were screwing with their heads."

"Yeah, well at least we all know what we've been doing this last month. You were so out of it, you nearly died on a lawn in Biwonga Road."

He protested. "I did not nearly die. I was just a bit hung-over, wasn't I, Tommo?"

Was he for real?

"No, Ed. You weren't just hung-over. You were drugged to the eyeballs and choking on your own spew." I didn't wait for an answer. "And by the way, not one of your Bombers mates came with me to help you out. They were too busy trying to get it on with Lena and Amy."

Casey shifted in his seat.

"What did you take, Ed?" I asked the question before he could point out that Casey had been just as absent.

"An E, I think. Marty didn't tell me what it was." He paused. "Oh, stop giving me the evil eye, Tommo. I know you warned me before. It's no big deal. I just had a bad reaction."

"But that's the problem, isn't it?" I challenged. "How can you tell before you try? And how can you be sure what you're getting is what someone says it is?" I asked.

Instinctively, Casey tag-teamed me. "And even if it is, how can you be sure you won't react badly to it next time?"

"Oh, come on, chill out. I'm clean now. I've got no choice. The police dobbed me in to the Bombers and I'm suspended from the Under Eighteens. Got an appointment with the Player Welfare officer on Friday." He blew his hair out of his eyes.

So the talk was true. I felt bad immediately and kind of responsible. Had I overreacted that night? How could his condition have been that serious if he was standing here six days later looking so healthy?

"You looked in a bad way, Ed. I had to call them."

Ed slapped my back. "No worries, Tommo. We're cool." He grabbed the other half of my sandwich and stuffed it in his mouth.

That's Ed for you. He has this amazing way of breaking everything down until it becomes totally simple.

"What do the Player Welfare people do?" I asked.

"I guess it depends on how much they want to keep me. They could terminate my contract right away, or they could help me out."

"How?" Casey asked.

"Sending me to a counsellor and making me do a drug awareness course. The club's got a policy on drugs and the National League does too. I guess I'll just have to wait and see."

"Let's hope they put you on a program then," I said.

"Don't you dare blow it if they give you a second chance," Casey ordered.

"I won't. I promise. If the Bombers let me play again, I'll pull my head in."

And then he took us on a trip to daydream land as only he could.

"Hey, what if I get really famous and I can just fly you two all around the country with me? Would you come to every game?"

"Yeah," Casey said.

They both looked at me.

"Hell, yeah!"

We laughed.

"So what's the deal with the chicks?" Ed asked.

"We totally screwed it up," Casey told him.

My mind flew back to Amy and me in the classroom doorway. My stomach flipped. I'd learned recently that it's OK to keep some stuff to yourself.

"Never mind. They're more trouble than they're worth," Ed said, snatching a piece of watermelon from my lunch box. "What's with the lunch box, Tommo?"

"Mum packed it," I said.

They both looked at me, aghast.

"I know. Since Saturday night she's been all over me like a rash." And she had been, despite the fact that she was still sulking about the Carrie Edwards thing.

They made sympathetic faces.

"Same here. Mum says she's never leaving me alone again and she reckons she's not buying me any more beer, either," Ed said.

Casey and I didn't bother answering him because Kieran Donnelly came ambling over.

"Hey." He nodded.

"What's up, Kieran?" Ed asked.

"Nothing, I just wanted to say, not everyone hates you."

"For what?"

"For wrecking the party."

"Thanks, man. We're stoked about that," Casey told him, his voice dripping sarcasm.

"It's mostly the girls who're still mad." He started to laugh.

"Hey, do you know what Rhona and Lena have arranged for tomorrow?"

We didn't try to guess.

"They're going to play paintball somewhere with half the girls in our form."

"So what?" I asked.

"Amy told Carla who told me they've printed off really big copies of your faces from this year's school photo and they're going to paste them to their safety helmets. Apparently yours was the most popular, Casey. Anyone who splats you between the eyes gets bonus points."

"Are they using my face too?" I was outraged. That couldn't be true.

He nodded. "But you'll be right. Romeo over there will cop most of the pain." He smiled at Casey.

"Can't believe they're using my face," I said.

"I think they're using all our faces," Kieran said.

"Didn't know you were tight with Dumb Carla." Casey made it sound like Kieran had just been caught eating his own snot.

Kieran ignored him. "Anyway, I just want to let you know there's no hard feelings, right?"

"Well, thanks for sharing that," Casey muttered as he left.

"At least he's still talking to us," Ed observed.

"He's a wanker," Casey growled.

"He's OK," I argued.

"I bet the paintball target thing was all Amy's idea," Casey said, changing the subject.

Ed was outraged. "Well, I think it's slack. Those chicks need to toughen up. So what if they got dumped in the end. They deserved it. You can't just get drunk and come on to guys in gardens and then scream when you change your mind."

My stomach lurched at the memory.

"Is that what Marty told you?"

"Yeah." He was sniggering.

"Robbie slapped Amy." I was trying to stay calm.

"Yeah, that was so not cool, but then again, she did kick him in the shins with those high heels. Why is there one rule for guys and another for girls?"

"Because guys are usually stronger, Ed," Casey answered before I could.

"Did he tell you they belted the crap out of me?" I asked.

"The way I heard it, you gave as good as you got."

"The girls were terrified, Ed. Your mates were out of control."

But he refused to believe me. "Nah, Marty said they were just mucking around. They've got careers to protect. They know that. Nothing would have happened in the end."

I didn't know any more. I couldn't trust my memory so there was no point in arguing about it now. It would just have to be a "no go" area for us and for sure I'd be keeping well out of his footy mates' way in future.

"Come on, you little nugget," he said holding me in a headlock, ruffling my hair. "Don't worry about them. They're cool with you. And don't feel sorry for chicks who are going off to splat our faces tomorrow in the park." He paused for a second, before adding, "I reckon we should make their revenge worthwhile."

"What do you mean?" I asked.

"Well, they've put a lot of effort into their little plan for Saturday, so let's give them something else to get mad about and make all that work with the photos worth it."

"By doing what?" Casey asked.

"What if…" Ed started.

I felt dread and excitement at the same time.

Casey groaned.

"What if we did an undies run through the playground right now? Show them that the boys don't give a shit. Show everyone. Remember Year Six?"

Casey spluttered. "Yeah, and we were well and truly in it afterwards. It's a good job it didn't go on our permanent record like my mum said it would. My whole family lived in fear for five months thinking this college would reject my application for Year Seven because of your undies stunt." He chucked away the crusts of his sandwich in disgust then hurried to pick them up off the gym floor and dropped them in the bin instead. I stifled a smile.

"My mum didn't even get to hear about it. I got all the letters before she did and threw them out," Ed said proudly. They looked at me expectantly.

"My parents grounded me, but I got up for a glass of water that night and I heard them laughing about it in Mum's study."

"That's why you'll be right when we do our run," Ed assured me.

"No way!" Casey said.

"We can't!" I protested, but Ed wouldn't be swayed.

"Come on. I know it would be even funnier if we did it with their photos on our dicks but the photocopying will take too long to organize."

"We can't!" I tried again.

Ed looked at me with an intensity I'd never seen before. "Tommo, everyone keeps saying I nearly died last Saturday night. It's part of my rehab therapy to do things that make me feel good. I'll tell Burrows the same thing when we get hauled in."

"Absolutely no way," I insisted.

"Come on. Think how funny it will be to hear all those stuck-up chicks screaming." He started to pull at his clothes.

I turned to Casey for support but his eyes were on fire. I hadn't seen him this alive in weeks.

"Casey, this is a very bad idea, mate."

I could see that I'd lost him already. They were stripping before my very eyes.

"Guys, our names are mud at the moment. This is so not the time to draw more attention to ourselves."

Ed chucked his shirt at me. "Are you in or out, pussy boy?"

Casey was already bouncing up and down in his white Bonds. He flashed me a huge grin and I recognized it immediately for what it was: redemption.

I stripped.

Ed shouted, "Three … two … one … GO!"

And we did. Speeding through the cold, empty corridors, we burst into the warmth of the winter sun. The sound of female screams in the yard was music to my ears.

Fifteen minutes later the corridor outside the Principal's office was still, the silence broken by the distinct sound of three sets of chattering teeth. Mrs Budd from the office came by and thoughtfully passed us a scratchy blue blanket from sick bay.

"Sorry, I've only got the one," she said, averting her eyes.

We accepted it gratefully and she scurried off.

"Stop hogging the blanket, Casey," Ed complained, pulling it towards him. Casey and I grabbed it back.

"It's not our fault you've been taking performance-enhancing drugs, hot shot," Casey said. "If your shoulders weren't so big, you'd have the same amount of blanket as us."

"Not if I was wrapping it round my dick. There'd be none left for you two then."

Air ballooned slowly in my stomach. It gushed through my body and burst in a geyser of sound, which rained down on Casey and Ed.

Mr Burrows's door flew open. "YOU'VE GOT TO BE KIDDING…"

I can't tell you what he said next. I couldn't hear him above the laughter of my mates.

Acknowledgements

Thanks to all the DE LA Boys out there, particularly those at De La Salle College, Caringbah, Sydney.

I'm grateful to Gary 'Boss' Burrows for conjuring time for me to write; to Steve Gough, my footy expert, to all the talented staff at De La who let me borrow their names and to the real Kieran Donnelly and Carrie Edwards for lending me theirs.

I owe a massive debt to my generous writing colleagues: Di Bates, Sandy Fussell, June Kier and also to everyone in Marg's CB gang.

Peter McFarlane, thanks for getting me started. It only took me nine years.

Bill Condon, thanks for always being just an email away. You know they won't stop coming, don't you?

Jackie Devlin, even in Canada you came through. You're a true friend.

To Sarah and the professional team at Walker Books, Australia, it's an honour to be one of your authors.

And finally, to my editor Sue Whiting, the Boofs and I know the story wouldn't have been the same without you. Thank you for all you have taught me. IOU.